MW01101698

**Here's what critics are saying about
Anna Snow's books:**

"Anna Snow does a great job at packing a lot into such a short story! If you like cozy mysteries with likable characters, *The Blonde Before Christmas* is the perfect story to curl up with this Christmas season!"
—Fresh Fiction

"This author knows suspense and how to place just the right amount of comedy to keep us reading. The combination is gripping and pulls a readers attention."
—Night Owl Reviews

"Will keep you spellbound until the very last page."
—The Romance Reviews

"A fast and enjoyable read, with plenty of emotion and passion."
—Dark Diva Reviews

BOOKS BY ANNA SNOW

Barb Jackson Mysteries:
Blondes' Night Out
(short story in the Killer Beach Reads collection)

The Blonde Before Christmas
(holiday short story)

Bubblegum Blonde

Other works:
Torque
All the Glittering Bones
Haunted Haven
My Sinful Valentine
Sinfully Delicious
Killer Kisses
Reluctant Angel
Guarding Eden
The Stranger Next Door
Tumbleweeds

BUBBLEGUM BLONDE

a Barb Jackson mystery

Anna Snow

BUBBLEGUM BLONDE
Copyright © 2015 by Anna Snow
Cover design by Estrella Designs

Published by Gemma Halliday Publishing
All Rights Reserved. Except for use in any review, the reproduction or
utilization of this work in whole or in part in any form by any electronic,
mechanical, or other means, now known or hereafter invented, including
xerography, photocopying and recording, or in any information storage and
retrieval system is forbidden without the written permission of the publisher,
Gemma Halliday.

This is a work of fiction. Names, characters, places, and incidents are either the
product of the author's imagination or are used fictitiously, and any
resemblance to actual persons, living or dead, business establishments, or
events or locales is entirely coincidental.

To all of my readers old and new, thank you from the bottom of my heart. I hope you enjoy Barb and the girls!
And to my husband, John. Thank you for being there for me when I need you and for helping me work things out when I've written myself into a corner. I love you.

CHAPTER ONE

———

It's entirely possible to have both boobs and a brain.

It's not like I'm walking, talking, sex-on-a-stick or anything, because really, I'm not. I'm just your typical, barely five-feet tall, a-little-too-curvy (due to my love of caramel macchiatos and pizza) girl next door. But for some reason, a blonde woman with a little extra in the chest area tends to throw off the opposite sex, especially when I mention that I'm a private investigator.

When I opened Jackson Investigations I never imagined how judgmental some people could be.

My PI firm wasn't a big affair like some of the other firms in town. I'd just finished my training and dumped a cheating ex when I opened the office. Financially, I was still a guppy in a tank full of sharks. But my company was slowly growing.

As far as employees went, my besties, Kelly and Mandy, were it. Mandy acted as receptionist and assistant, while Kelly worked cases with me. She'd often go undercover to bust a cheating spouse without a second thought.

We'd been hard at work trying to make a name for the company for close to three years now, but so far the only cases we'd been trusted with were your run-of-the-mill cheaters. Still, I couldn't complain. These clients might not be high profile or bring in bank, but they paid the bills…barely.

Despite only making just enough to pay the light bill, I wouldn't trade my job for anything in the world. I loved what I did, even if it meant eating ramen noodles a few nights a week.

A knock sounded. Then my office door opened a few inches.

"Barb, there's someone here to see you."

I glanced up from the screen I'd been staring at for what felt like a century and spotted Kelly closing the office door behind her. Kelly was loud, sarcastic, and wonderful. She was a great girl and my all-time best friend. We'd met when I first opened the business three years ago and over the years had become so close an industrial-sized crowbar couldn't pry us apart. She was brilliant, witty, and didn't take crap from anyone.

I wanted to be Kelly when I grew up.

Kelly was tall and thin, sported a number of tattoos, loved the color black, and was amazingly pretty with her own set of full lips, high cheekbones, and short black hair.

She had men falling at her feet, while I stared at my feet when confronted by a handsome man. She was the polar opposite of my petite, slightly round, blonde self. But the physical differences never mattered to us.

We were *sistahs from anotha mistah*.

Her words, not mine.

"Who is it?" I blinked my eyes in an attempt to bring the room around me back into focus. Watching a surveillance camera did a number on a sleep-deprived person's eyes. At the moment I wondered if I'd ever get my vision back to normal.

I blinked and then rubbed my palms against my closed eyes.

"How should I know? I'm not Miss Cleo." Kelly shrugged with one palm pointed toward the sky.

Did I happen to mention that Kelly took sarcasm to a whole new level?

I slowly opened my eyes and cocked a brow at her.

"He said his name is Jason King and that he needs to speak directly to you about his situation." She air-quoted the word *situation*, which told me that she thought this guy was a total tool.

"That's about all he would tell me. He's determined to see you and a bit of an arrogant ass, if I do say so myself."

"You didn't tell him that he's an ass, did you?"

She smiled sweetly. "No, but the night's still young." She pressed her black-framed glasses up her pert nose with the tip of her index finger and waited for my response.

I shook my head. "You're a handful, you know that?"

She nodded. The smile never left her face.

I bit my bottom lip. "Jason King," I said while trying to dredge up where I'd heard the name before, but nothing came to me. "The name sounds familiar, but I can't place it right off the top of my head. Did you recognize him at all?"

She shrugged her shoulders. "Nope." She shook her head. "He looks just like every other businessman in this town."

I'd lived in the city since conception, and at times all the businessmen milling about appeared carbon copied.

Suits, ties, shiny black shoes, and there was often either a shiny bald head framed by thinning white hair or a full head of over-gelled hair sitting on their shoulders. Neither of which I found the least bit attractive, but hey, whatever floats their boats, right? The look obviously did something for the gorgeous women on their arms. Or maybe it was their money not their appearance the women found attractive. Who knew?

"Do you know if I have any other appointments today, Kelly?" I asked.

"Nope. I checked the schedule book before I came in here. You're all clear today. You're only supposed to review some tapes and return a few calls," she answered.

This mystery guy had piqued my interest, so I relented.

"All right, I'll see him since I have some time, but I want you in here on this one. Who knows what this guy's story is." I looked up at the clock and found that it was only a little after ten o'clock in the morning. "Follow him in please."

Kelly gave me a two-finger—which was much more polite than her one usual finger—salute and left the room.

I stopped the surveillance disk I'd been reviewing for a client and powered off my monitor, then leaned back in my oversized desk chair and frowned.

I'd already seen all that I needed to see on the disk in order to know the guy I'd been tailing for the last week was cheating on his wife. The last thing I needed was for some busybody to come in my office, take a look at the computer monitor, and see his bare bum bent over the hood of a car before I told his wife that her husband was indeed having an affair with his assistant…his very male assistant.

"Jason King. Jason King. Jason King." I repeated the name as I tapped my bottom lip with the tip of my pen. I tried like crazy to figure out why that name sounded so familiar, but nothing came to me. I couldn't pin the name to a face.

If I'd had time, I would've done a quick Google search, but Mr. Pushy was already in the lobby demanding an audience. That alone was enough to make me consider telling the guy to hit the road, but like I said before, I had bills to pay, and just because the guy was pushy didn't mean I could tell him to hit the road before I met him. I have to admit my curiosity was a big deciding factor for meeting him.

My Aunt Mona often warned me that curiosity killed the cat, but I couldn't ever seem to help myself. When a puzzle presented itself, I had to solve it.

A few moments later, Kelly opened the door, and the bottom dropped out of my happy little world.

"Barb."

My legs shook. I stood slowly and stared into the eyes of the one man who'd always sent my brain flying out the window.

"Jason?"

We stared at each other, taking in the other's appearance for what felt like a silent eternity. He was the same as I remembered, tall, with a broad chest, brown eyes, and perfectly auburn hair. For a moment all those old feelings, the ones I'd shoved in a drawer in the deepest, darkest, better-off-forgotten recesses of my mind, came rushing back. It took everything I had in me to squash those damaging feelings before they roared back to life and consumed me all over again.

Jason and I had ended more than five years ago, and I had no interest in reviving that little misstep of my life. That relationship was one of those times when I should've listened to my dear, sweet, nosy-as-all-get-out Aunt Mona and run in the opposite direction. She saw Jason for what he was. A liar and a cheater. I, on the other hand, only saw a hot, successful man who was interested in me.

I'd been an idiot, and no matter what he was selling, I definitely wasn't buying.

"You're Jason. You're Barb, and I'm Kelly." Kelly interrupted the moment. A grin spread across her face. "I thought you didn't know him."

It took a minute for me to regain my bearings, but I finally found my words. "I don't. I do. I did," I stuttered. "We knew each other a long time ago," I reluctantly admitted.

"And you just forgot his name?" Kelly looked at me like I'd sprouted a second head.

"No." I frowned at her. "When I knew him, his name was Jason Charles. Not Jason King." Jason's mother had kept her maiden name when she married. I guess that's why his name change had seemed so familiar. I just hadn't picked up on the reason why before he walked through my door.

He chose that moment to break out the gorgeous boyish smile that could melt a woman's panties in two seconds flat. The urge to slap him for even thinking about walking back into my life like nothing had ever happened, for that sensational smile that had always had the power to do me in, rolled through me. But instead of smacking him, I listened to what he had to say. I needed to know what he wanted from me because there was no doubt that he wanted something.

"I started using my mother's maiden name when I opened my business."

I cocked an eyebrow at him in question.

"I'm sure you heard about my father's misstep a few years ago," he half explained.

"Misstep? Do you mean the embezzlement accusations? I'd say that was more than a misstep."

"Call it what you want. No one is going to want to do business with an accountant whose family has a history of embezzlement. So, I changed my last name," he said with a slight shrug.

"Makes sense if you want clients," I said with a nod.

"And we *knew each other* seems a bit mild, doesn't it, Barb? After all, we *were engaged* for more than a year," he said with a frown.

"Engaged?" Kelly gaped and looked back and forth between the two of us. "You were engaged to *him*?" She pointed at Jason where he stood, still leaning against the doorframe.

"It's a long story." I pinched the bridge of my nose. "One I absolutely do *not* care to repeat," I hedged.

I caught Kelly gaping at me out of the corner of my eye. I decided that if I was that transparent I needed to get my stuff together. There was no way on planet Earth I would allow this guy to get under my skin. Not again. I'd been burned by Jason once before, and I wasn't about to let it happen a second time.

I tamped down the old feelings threatening to bubble up inside me at just the sight of him and regained my composure.

"Well"—I released a pent up breath—"I have to assume that you're here for a reason. Have a seat, and we'll get started."

I directed him toward one of the chocolate-brown leather chairs situated before my cluttered desk and took my seat. Kelly situated herself and her notepad in the matching chair next to Jason's.

Yes, I said notepad. Kelly was what one would call technologically challenged. She was the complete opposite of my receptionist and dear friend Mandy. Kelly's last attempt at using an iPad to help me with research wound up with her neck-deep in the depths of a nudist site for the elderly. She'd sworn off electronics until further notice.

Jason glanced over at her, then back at me. "I was kind of hoping we could speak in private."

"Anything you have to say to me you can say in front of Kelly. She's my assistant, so she's going to hear all of the ins and outs as to why you're here anyway."

He cleared his throat and cast another furtive glance at Kelly, then back at me. "I understand that, but I'd feel more comfortable speaking to you alone this first meeting. Please, Barb? This is important."

For the love of… Enough with the puppy dog eyes already. I was afraid that if he kept batting those obscenely long lashes at me he was going to take flight.

The last thing I wanted was to be alone with Jason, but if shooing Kelly from the room was the only way to get what he wanted out of him so he could hurry up and be on his way, then so be it.

Kelly gave me an almost-imperceptive nod.

"Um, sure. Kelly, its fine. I can handle this."

Kelly winked at me and left the room. She knew the moment that he left my office I'd tell her everything he said anyway. We didn't keep secrets from each other, except the one sitting before me, but as I said before, he was a part of my past I had no desire to dredge up.

The second the door closed behind her I knew I was in trouble.

"I've missed you."

"Is that why you're here? Because if it is, you're wasting your time." I ignored the needy look in his eyes.

"Time with you is never wasted."

Boy, was he full of crap or what?

"That's obviously not what you thought when we were together, or you wouldn't have spent your every waking moment on top of your secretary."

"I apologized for that." He frowned. "I was immature, stupid even. I'm different now."

Different?

Yeah, and the sky was red, wine was nasty-stinky-poo-poo water, and turkey bacon tasted better than the real thing.

Different, my butt. The only thing that appeared different about Jason was that it looked like he'd lightened his hair color half a shade.

"Jason, is this why you're here? To rehash our past? If it is, then I'm going to have to ask you to leave. I have work to do, and our past relationship is a part of my life I'd rather never again revisit."

I started to stand. Jason held up a hand to stop me.

"No, that's not why I'm here," he said quickly. "I really do need your help, Barb. This is serious."

I took in his expression. He really did look like he was having a hard time. Against my better judgment I sat back down and asked, "What exactly do you need my help with that's so serious? What's going on? Are you in some kind of trouble?"

He released what sounded like a frustrated sigh and ran his hand through his normally immaculate hair. For the first time since he'd walked into my office, I studied him. He looked exhausted. Faint bags sat dark beneath his tired brown eyes. His hair was slightly disheveled, his body strung tight with tension, and his dress shirt and black slacks were starting to rumple. The man seated before me with his less-than-perfect appearance was not the Jason I knew. Something was definitely up. But did I really want to know what was causing his distress? Did I want to step in the middle of whatever he'd gotten himself into? Because if he was in fact in the middle of something nefarious, there was no doubt in my mind that he'd gotten *himself* into it.

I didn't want to find myself mixed up in any of Jason's schemes.

Were I a vain, conceited woman, I would've let myself believe that his tension was due to the fact that he was sitting across from me, a woman he was lucky to have had but screwed over and lost...but I wasn't that kind of girl. As much as I sometimes wished I was that girl, I just wasn't.

"Jason?" I prodded.

"Yeah. Kind of."

"Care to elaborate?" I pressed. "Because in my line of work, *kind of* doesn't cut the cake."

"You know I started my own accounting firm four years ago?" He leaned his elbows on his knees.

"Yes." I nodded. If there was one thing Jason was good with, it was numbers.

"I do a lot of business for individuals as well as some larger companies. One of those companies in particular being Hatchett Enterprises."

"Hatchett?" I interrupted. "As in modeling mogul Robert Hatchett?"

Robert Hatchett owned and operated the biggest modeling agencies in the United States. His models were everywhere—television, movies, magazines, and billboards. Hatchett was *the* name in modeling. If you wanted to be the next Naomi Campbell, Hatchett Enterprises was the agency you tried to land.

"The one and only."

"That's a pretty big deal," I said. "How'd that happen?"

"Mr. Hatchett came into my office six months ago, chatted me up, said he heard great things about me from a colleague, and hired me on the spot to work as his personal accountant. The money he offered was just too good to pass up."

"I can imagine." I shook my head. "Personal accounts? As in illegal?" I asked.

"No, no, nothing like that." He waved a hand in the air. "The modeling agency has its own accounting company, due to the fact that it's a multi-million-dollar business. All agency accounts are dealt with by another firm, but Hatchett has more going on than the modeling agency. He has charities and such, and that's what he hired me to keep track of."

"Sounds complicated."

That whole set up was way too complicated for me. I could barely balance my checkbook. Not that there was a lot of money in my account to balance to begin with. I was, at the moment, what I liked to call *financially challenged.*

"It can be at times," he agreed. "The other firm that takes care of the Hatchett Modeling accounts and I meet once a month to go over the numbers just to make sure we're on the same page, and there're no loose ends. The last thing we want to do is get Hatchett or ourselves into some kind of financial trouble because of oversights. No one wants to deal with the IRS."

Amen, brother.

"Wait." I held up a hand to stop him. "Wasn't Robert Hatchett's wife murdered in their home about two weeks ago?"

At least that's what I thought I'd heard on the bits of the evening news I'd been able to catch. In my line of work, I wasn't home much, so television watching was sparse.

"That's why I'm here."

Why did I have the feeling that the shiznit was about to hit the fan? Oh, that's right, because wherever Jason went, crap always seemed to start flying. It was like he had his own troop of poo-flinging monkeys following him everywhere he went. I briefly considered carrying an umbrella to keep myself from being splattered.

Over the last three years as a private investigator I'd learned that most cases always lead back to one of two things, money or sex. Sometimes both. Most of the time, a spouse suspected their significant other of cheating simply based on behavior, such as not wanting to make love, or their money didn't add up.

Money or sex.

With Jason, I had a sinking feeling that I already knew which of the two had landed him in trouble.

"Were you having an affair with Mrs. Hatchett?"

Yeah, it was crass of me to ask, but I had to know. I felt the need to get that little tidbit out of the way.

He rolled his eyes and leaned back against the seat. "No. I wasn't banging Lydia. Jesus, Barb." He glared at me. "I cheated once. It was a mistake. Let it go already. It's not like I sleep with every woman who walks by."

Could've fooled me.

I bit my tongue to keep from telling him to go straight to hell on the first bus out. Instead, I motioned for him to continue. When it came to sleeping with a woman, no matter what he told me, I wouldn't believe it. If the woman was willing, Jason was all too happy to oblige. Instead of nagging him about his relationship with Lydia Hatchett, I let the subject drop for now.

"The day her body was found at her place the police called me in for questioning. They released me a few hours later. Three days after the initial questioning a detective paid a visit to my office. He asked some more questions and informed me that from that point on, I was being considered a suspect."

"A murder suspect?"

"Yeah. Imagine my surprise." He shook his head.

I leaned my elbows on the desk, unable to control my rising curiosity. "What kind of questions did the detective ask you?"

"How well I knew Lydia. Were we having an affair? Had I ever done any kind of personal work for her that her husband didn't know about? Stuff like that, which were basically the same questions I'd been asked days before at the station. I contacted my attorney. He said that without any hard evidence against me, I was *probably* safe, but *probably* isn't good enough for me."

"You said that the cops don't have any hard evidence against you, but they have to have something or else they wouldn't name you as a suspect," I said as I tapped the end of a pen with my thumb. "So what do they have?"

He looked away.

"Jason? Do the cops have any evidence pointing to you or not?"

He blew out a breath. "Yes."

"What do they have?"

He cleared his throat. "They found my jacket and money clip in her bedroom."

"Your jacket and money clip? I thought you said you weren't sleeping with her." I raised one eyebrow. "If you weren't sleeping with Lydia, how did those things come to be in her bedroom, the bedroom where she was murdered, at all?"

In my line of work someone didn't lose such personal items in a married woman's bedroom unless they were mattress-surfing with said woman. Which, knowing Jason, wasn't that unlikely.

"I think I'm being framed. That's why I need your help."

"Who would want to frame you for murder?" I asked. "You're an accountant. You said that you're not into any illegal dealings, so why would someone try to frame you for murder?"

"I don't know. That's why I'm here."

"Do you have an alibi for the time of the murder?" I tapped my bottom lip with my pen.

"I was home alone." He shook his head. "I know it's weak, but surely one of the neighbors saw my car in the drive or something."

"That's a long shot that won't stand up in court. Just because someone saw your car in the drive doesn't mean that you were home. That story won't fly with anyone."

He ran his fingers through his hair. "I know it won't, but it's all I have. I was home the night she was killed. I swear."

"Swear all you want, but that alibi won't hold up."

I leaned back in my chair and tapped the end of my pen on the desk as I thought. This was a tricky situation. One that could land me in a huge heap of trouble if I didn't play my cards right. There was no way on Earth I was going to interfere with an ongoing murder investigation any further than I was legally allowed, but my curiosity was getting the best of me.

"Jason, this is an ongoing murder investigation." I set the pen down and tapped the desk with my index finger, a habit I had when thinking. "I can only look into a case up to a certain point without stepping outside the bounds of legality."

Which was the truth. While I could snoop around and ask questions, I had to do so without interfering with the investigation the police were conducting. I would have to walk a very thin line if I took this case.

"I'm not asking you to interfere or do anything illegal," he said quickly. "I'm asking you to conduct your own investigation."

"Which is exactly what I just said." I rolled my eyes. "But tell me something, Jason. Why should I help you?" I asked. "I can't think of a single solitary thing that you've ever been honest with me about." I flopped back in my cushy chair. "Why should I believe that you're innocent?"

"Because I am," he said.

I narrowed my eyes at him. As much as I disliked Jason, I had a hard time believing he was capable of murder. He just didn't have it in him.

"You're asking me to delve into a murder. A high-profile murder that the cops are currently investigating. I can do it, but you have to understand that this is a tricky situation for me and my girls. One wrong move, one step over the line, and we could be in trouble right alongside you, and in case you're unaware, prison orange is not my color. Do you see where I'm going with this?"

While I really wasn't afraid of getting thrown in jail, I *was* concerned about what exactly I could do to help him. I usually dealt with cheaters, liars, and the occasional thief. Murderers were a whole new crop of crazy that I had little experience with.

"Please, Barb," he begged. "I need help with this, and you're the only one I can trust right now. I didn't kill Lydia Hatchett. You have to help me. I'm desperate."

Good gravy, if there was one thing I couldn't stand, it was the sight of a man begging. Despite his cheating, Jason was a good man. (Well, he had been at one time.) He was honest. (Somewhat. That was still kind of a sketchy area with the cheating and all.) But despite my personal feelings about him, I had a gut feeling that he was actually innocent. If there was one thing I'd learned in my thirty years of life, it was to trust my gut.

I knew taking this case was a bad idea. I also knew that this was the case that could either make me or break me because Hatchett was an important man, and this was a popular case.

There was also the small matter of if I turned this job down and Jason really was innocent, then an innocent man would be sitting in prison for the rest of his life because I was too afraid to get involved.

Could I afford to let the case that could make my company the biggest in the city slip through my fingers? The only thing I could do was put on my big-girl panties and bite the bullet, so to speak. Kelly was so going to kick me right in the rear for getting us into such a situation, but a girl's gotta do what a girl's gotta do, and I knew my girls would have my back no matter what decision I made.

This single case could put Jackson Investigations on the map, and I might be able to pay the light bill on time next month, which was a rare occurrence as of late. Last month I'd actually considered sending them an IOU with a pic of Kelly in a bikini as payment and hope they left the power on.

I reached into my top desk drawer, pulled out a piece of my favorite watermelon Bubblicious, and popped it into my mouth.

Some people smoked. Some drank. I chewed bubblegum.

"I'll do it," I said and nearly choked on the words as they passed my lips. "On one condition."

"You name it," he said and scooted to the edge of his seat, hope evident in his shining eyes.

"From this point on, you never lie to me. If I ask you a question for information, anything at all, you tell me the truth. No exceptions. I don't care how bad it might make you look, how scandalous it may be, or who besides you it involves—you tell me exactly what I need to know. It isn't just your butt on the line anymore, and I'll be dipped in the sewer before I let you drag me down with you."

"I swear," he answered quickly. "Thank you, Barb. You don't know how much this means to me."

"I think I might," I muttered as I stood. I already felt the weight of the world resting on my shoulders.

I circled the desk and held out my hand for a handshake before I could come to my senses and change my mind. I was more than a little surprised when Jason jumped to his feet, reached out, and pulled me into his arms in a tight embrace.

I stood still, in total shock until his scent hit me. The fragrance of his musky aftershave and the natural scent of his skin enveloped me. My inner hoochie took over, and I let myself melt into him.

I know, I know, it was a seriously bad move, but give a girl a break. My love life had been practically nonexistent for the past year, and sad to say, I'd been head over heels in love with Jason at one time…until he betrayed me.

I felt him press his lips against the top of my head.

Oh, God! Not that! Not the tender, you're so-special head kiss! Abort! Abort!

I forced myself to pull away before things got really out of hand, and I did something stupid like let my hormones take over. There was no way on Heaven or Earth I was going back down that road again. That sucker was full of potholes.

"I'll get started today and call you if I find anything."

He smiled and some of the tension visibly lifted from his body. "I don't know how I'll ever repay you."

"I do." I smiled and turned back to my desk, then pressed the intercom button.

"Yes?" Kelly's voice echoed in the room between us.

"Mr. King will be paying you for our services on his way out. Charge him the cheating-arrogant-fool rate."

"You got it, boss," she answered, and I could hear the grin in her voice.

Jason chuckled and shook his head as he strode to the door and grasped the knob.

"Same ol' Barb."

He grinned once more at me over his shoulder and exited my office.

I shrugged because, really, what could I say? He was right. I was the same ol' Barb, and I was happy with that.

I just hoped he wasn't the same old Jason, because if he was, he'd be sitting in big-boy jail by the end of the week, and I'd be back to not being able to pay the light bill.

CHAPTER TWO

"You agreed to do what?"

I cringed at the deadly look Kelly cast me from across the desk.

If looks could kill, I'd be dead with a capital D.

"I know you're angry, and you have every right to be, but I couldn't just let him walk out of here knowing that he may very well be innocent.

She continued to look at me with a, *you-expect-me-to-believe-that* expression.

"Seriously, Kelly, could you live with yourself if you knew an innocent man was spending life in prison because you were too afraid to help him?"

She scrunched up her nose and pursed her lips. "No," she finally admitted. "But is that the real reason you agreed to help him? Or is it because you two used to be engaged? *Which*, by the way," she wagged her finger at me, "I'm still pissed you didn't tell me about." She flipped me off.

Maybe some of the reason I wanted to help Jason was because of our past. Maybe a small part of me wanted to prove to him that I was good at this private investigating thing, which was something he always laughed at me for dreaming about. But I'd never admit it.

I groaned. "I'm sorry I didn't tell you about Jason. We happened before I opened the office. Besides, it's not like our relationship is something that I like to remember." I shrugged and tried to explain. "I loved him. He loved to roll around with other women. I'm completely over him. End of story."

And I was. Getting over Jason took a while, several bottles of wine, and a few sappy chick flicks, but after all this time, I really was over him.

"And this is the same guy you put our rears on the line for because you think he's innocent? How can you trust him after what he did to you?"

I shrugged one shoulder. "I feel it in my gut. Besides, he cheated on me, he didn't sell me out to the mob or something."

She pursed her red lips. "I don't know, Barb. This case, it sounds like more trouble than it's worth. What if he's lying?"

"I know," I admitted, "but just think about it, Kelly. This case, if we can crack it, could make us. Can you imagine what kind of cases people would bring to us if we discovered who really killed Lydia Hatchett? We wouldn't have to hunt cheaters all day everyday just to make ends meet."

"Chasing cheaters is sort of fun. We get to see all kinds of crazy stuff." Kelly grinned.

I rolled my eyes but kept my mouth shut because she was right. Busting a cheater could be exciting, and you never knew what you were going to see.

We'd seen some things I still couldn't get out of my head. There were just some things a person could never unsee.

"But"—she sighed and shook her head—"I'll do whatever you need me to do. We need to be extra careful with this one. Make sure we dot our I's and cross our T's. The last thing we want is the police department thinking that we're stepping on their toes and shutting us down."

"You don't have to remind me," I said and meant every word. The last place I wanted to end up because of a shifty ex-boyfriend was in the slammer…or labor and delivery, but that's a completely different story.

"So, where should we start?" she asked.

I spat my now-flavorless bubblegum in the trashcan, then immediately popped a new piece in my mouth.

"I think we need to start by digging into the pasts of Robert and Lydia Hatchett and Jason as well. We need to get a peek at their financials, anything they might have had their thumbs into, pending deals, and so on, in case Lydia was the victim of some deal gone wrong."

"Done." Kelly made a note on the yellow legal pad she held.

I still wasn't used to Kelly's lack of tech knowledge. She still used an ancient-looking flip phone that had definitely seen better days...in the nineties.

"I'll call up Mandy. If anyone can find that info, it's her."

"Perfect." I nodded. "I know it's her day off, but we could really use her help."

I grabbed my cell phone and dialed the number to the local police department.

"What are you doing?" Kelly asked.

"Calling the police station to see if by some chance I can see the police report or at least get *some* information on the case."

"You think they'll let you see the file?" Kelly raised her eyebrows.

"If this were a simpler case, yeah, but with this one being high profile, no." I shook my head. "But it can't hurt to try. The worst they can do is tell me no, then I'm right back where we started."

She nodded and continued to dial Mandy's number while I waited for the police station to pick up.

On the third ring a perky dispatcher answered. "Police Department. This is Tiffany. How can I help you?"

"This is Barb Jackson of Jackson Investigations. I need to speak with the detective in charge of the Lydia Hatchett case."

"Sure. Let me see if he's in. Just one moment."

The dispatcher put me on hold, and a second later, the worst elevator version of Billy Idol's "Rebel Yell" I'd ever heard filled my ears. I had the fleeting thought that whoever had the brilliant idea to destroy that song needed a swift kick in the rump.

At least five minutes passed before a deep voice finally came over the line.

"Detective Black. What can I do for you?"

"I'm Barb Jackson of Jackson Investigations. I'd like to speak to you about the Lydia Hatchett case."

"What about it?"

He was quite brusque, but I brushed it off. He was a detective. He had a lot on his plate.

"Well, for starters," I began, "I've been approached by someone concerning the case. I'd like to see the case file if possible to aid in my investigation."

"No can do. Sorry."

"I understand that this is an ongoing investigation, but I've been hired to look into this case as well. I'm sure you can understand and extend a little bit of professional courtesy."

"Listen, lady, I get that you're a private investigator and all, but this is an ongoing murder investigation. At this point I'm not willing to show anyone this file." I heard the snap of what sounded like a heavy folder hitting the desk. "So I'm sorry, but no. There's no way you're getting your hands on the case file."

His bluntness started to rub me the wrong way. I was doing my best to be polite, but he was making it rough.

"I understand how important this case is," I said, "but my client—"

"I can only imagine who your client is, seeing as how there's only one suspect in the case." He huffed out a breath. "Just in case you didn't hear me, this is an ongoing murder case. I can't tell you not to conduct your little investigation, but I can tell you to stay out of my way. Don't tamper with anything, and I mean anything, or I'll toss you in a cell. Understand?"

"Yeah, I got it. Thanks for your consideration," I said with all the sarcasm I could muster and ended the call. It was times like this that I longed for an old phone. I just didn't get the same satisfaction pressing the end-call button as I did when I slammed down a receiver.

"So, I'm guessing that was a no go?" Kelly asked.

"He was an ass," I said. "It looks like we'll have to do this the old fashioned way." I smiled. The thought of digging in and really investigating sent a thrill through me that I hadn't felt since my days training to be a private investigator.

Since some of the information we needed was private and could only be obtained with a warrant that we didn't have and couldn't get, and the cop who could share it with us was refusing to play nice and give me a peek at the goods, we needed a top-notch hacker to get us what we needed.

"Mandy said she'll be here in twenty minutes."

"Great," I said and grabbed my purse.

Mandy Willow was the best computer hacker I'd ever seen. If anyone could get their hands on Hatchett's financial records, it was Mandy.

Her brother, Ron, who—sad to say—was serving five to ten in the state pen for hacking into the wrong companies' files, taught her how to hack into just about anything.

While Mandy could do anything with a computer, when it came to working in the field, she was our last resort. She froze up worse than a mobster at confession, which left stakeouts and face-to-face meetings to Kelly and me.

"I'm going down to the station to see if I can get a look at the case file."

"Didn't that detective just tell you that you couldn't see it?"

"Yes, but Aunt Mona might have overheard something about the case, and if I play my cards right, I might be able to sneak in and get a look for myself." It was a long shot, but I had to try. "I know Mandy wouldn't have a problem hacking into the system while she's checking out Hatchett's bank accounts, but I want to do as much of this legally as possible. If I can't see the file, then I'll have Mandy hack the station's system as a last resort. In the meantime, do you think you can handle Googling the case and gathering as much information as you can from the media coverage? There might be something useful mixed in with all of the extra hooey they add to pad the story."

Kelly nodded. "Mandy taught me how to Google. I'm on it."

I wasn't too convinced that Kelly could handle the Googling, but I had to hope that when I got back to the office the computer wouldn't be damaged beyond repair.

Kelly was known to have an extremely short fuse.

Grabbing my keys, I headed out the door and called over my shoulder, "Let Mandy know what I need when she gets in, and let's get this show on the road."

"You got it, boss."

I hurried across the sidewalk and slid into the driver seat of my car. I started the ignition and pulled out onto the road and in the direction of the police station. I was in a hurry to get this case over and done with.

The sooner Jason King was out of my life the better.

* * *

The police station itself was a three-story, concrete structure with tinted windows and revolving doors at the entry.

I pulled up next to the curb outside the station and killed the ignition. I really didn't feel like being subjected to that little metal detector wand being passed over my body or explaining to some befuddled door guard why exactly I was carrying a gun, so I slid my weapon from the waist of my jeans and locked it in the glove compartment. Besides, if I wasn't safe in a building full of cops, I wasn't safe anywhere.

With a final check of myself in the visor mirror, I ran my fingers through my wavy blonde hair, got out of the car, and locked the doors.

The afternoon sun shone down on me like a spotlight as I made my way across the sidewalk and up the steps. I could already feel what little bit of makeup I wore starting to melt right off my face. Even though the seasons were changing and the days were becoming shorter, it was unusually hot.

The air-conditioned building called my name, and I put a little hustle in my step to get out of the midday heat before I was nothing but a sweaty puddle on the ground.

I pushed my way through the revolving doors leading into the station and breathed a sigh of relief as a gust of cool air washed over me.

The officer stationed at the door eyed me then stood up and stepped in front of the metal detector. He was heavyset and looked nearly as enthused about getting up to run my bag through the machine as I was to be in the station at all. I'd much rather have been back at the office, but instead here I was, possibly about to do something illegal.

The officer motioned for me to put my purse on the conveyer belt, so I did and then walked through the metal detector without incident. Once through the detector I reclaimed my purse. The officer was staring at the little bit of cleavage beneath the V-neck of my T-shirt with a creepy grin. I groaned, tossed my purse strap over my shoulder, and continued across the lobby. I didn't have time to tell him that he was a pig. I kind of figured that he already knew and just didn't care.

The precinct was bustling with activity, but to my surprise, the front desk looked fairly clear, so I made my way over.

"Barb! Long time no see!"

I smiled at the older woman behind the desk. "Mona, how's it going?"

"It'd be going a lot better if it was quitting time, I can tell you that. We're running shorthanded today, so I'm down here from the chief's office helping Tiffany out." She grinned. "We've been busier than a beehive." She shook her head. "But it's slowed down a little bit over the last few minutes. These people are just waiting for one of the boys in the back to come handle their problems."

Mona was the chief's receptionist but often helped at the front desk when the precinct was shorthanded.

"I still think I should apologize beforehand, because my being here is just going to add to your workload," I said with a smile and shook my head.

I'd known Mona all of my life. She was my favorite aunt's best friend, and after my aunt and mother passed away in a car accident, Mona made it known that she was from that day forward assuming the role of auntie.

I had absolutely zero complaints.

She narrowed her green eyes at me, pursed her bright-red lips, and then leaned her thin arms on the counter. She looked around discreetly. "Is there something you're needing me to help you with?" she asked in a soft voice.

"I should've called ahead, but I'm in a hurry." I nodded. "I need to get into the back and see if I can sneak a peek at the case file on Lydia Hatchett."

Mona's eyes widened, and she blew out a breath. "What in the world do you need to see that case file for? I thought peeping Toms and slimy spouses were more your thing?"

"They usually are," I admitted. "But this morning a client came into the office and hired me to clear him of her murder. I need some place to start, and getting a good look at that file would be a great place."

"Someone hired you to investigate her murder?" she asked with a shocked expression.

"I'm a little hurt that you find someone thinking that I can solve a murder an impossibility." I placed my hands on my hips. "But yes. He thinks he's being framed, and I happen to believe him."

"I don't think that about you at all. I know you can solve any case thrown your way. I think you're the best private investigator there is, but I don't know, Barb. This is a dangerous case. A woman was murdered, and you usually deal with cheaters…"

Mona always had my best interests at heart. She worried about me like I was her own child, so I often understood her lack of enthusiasm where my career was concerned.

"Mona, I know that this isn't my typical case, but this is the one that could put my company on the map. You know how hard I've been trying to make a name for myself. For my company." I leaned my forearms on the counter again and lowered my voice. "If I can uncover who really killed Lydia Hatchett, I could free an innocent man *and* put a murderer behind bars. I've already taken the case, so I'm going to do all that I can to solve this murder. I could really use your help."

"Being a private investigator you have privileges here, why don't you just ask to see it?"

"I tried, but when I called this morning and asked to see the case file the detective heading up the investigation wouldn't budge."

Mona looked at me for a long moment. Her bright-red eyebrows lowered in a frown that matched the one on her lips. Mona was always worried that I'd go off and get myself killed.

"All right, here's what we're going to do," she said with a sigh. "I can't let you back there. It's too big of a risk. If one of the officers saw you wandering around unsupervised you'd be busted in a heartbeat. Then we'd both be in a heap of trouble."

"But Mona—"

"Just listen." She held up a hand to stop any further argument. "You might stick out like a sore thumb, but I won't.

Let me go back there and see what I can do, but you promise me that you won't go off and get yourself killed if I can get you the information you need."

See what I mean?

"I can't let you do that, Mona," I argued. "Do you have any idea how much trouble you'd be in if you got caught with that file?"

There was no way I was going to let her get into any kind of trouble because of me and this case. It would be easier to just have Mandy hack the system. At least then if I were to get caught, I would take the fall, not Mona or the girls.

"It just so happens that I do," she said. "But this is my decision. Wait right here."

She waved a hand at the chairs along the far wall. "Hang out for a few minutes, and let me see what I can come up with, but I can't make any promises."

"Be careful, Mona."

Mona turned to talk to the other woman, who I assumed was the Tiffany I'd spoken with when I'd called earlier. I looked around and spotted an empty seat near the wall and made my way over. A moment later, I watched as Mona opened a heavy metal door leading to the main floor of the station and then disappeared from sight.

The crowded station finally started to thin out, but I still felt restless, so I stood and paced for a few minutes. When that did nothing to ease my nervous jitters I leaned my back against the cool wall and sighed. I had no idea how long it would take Mona to get the file I needed, but I hoped it wouldn't be long. I could hang out in the lobby only so long before I drew attention and someone started asking questions.

I pulled my phone from my jeans pocket to check my text messages and found one from Mandy.

At the office. Already digging.

Although I knew Kelly had already told her where I was and what I was doing, I fired off a quick response telling her that I was at the station and that I'd be back soon, then slipped the phone back into my purse.

Nearly ten minutes had passed, and there was still no sign of Mona. I was starting to worry. If she was caught she'd lose her job or worse, which was why I didn't want her to go after the file herself. The thought of my favorite aunt jeopardizing her job and possibly risking jail time churned my stomach.

I found myself staring at the metal door Mona had disappeared behind as though my willing her to appear would work. If it actually did, I was going to start willing myself to win the lottery and lose thirty pounds.

"Miss? Are you waiting for someone?"

The deep, whiskey-and-honey, smooth sound of a man's voice yanked me out of my lottery-deep, tiny-waisted thoughts. I glanced up in search of whom the voice came from and was pleasantly surprised.

The man standing before me was, in one word, *hot*.

He stood well over six feet tall, was muscular with a broad chest and shoulders, a slim waist, and thick muscular legs. He wore a tight, midnight-blue T-shirt and distressed jeans, both of which fit him like a glove, accentuating the dips and lines of his muscles as he moved toward me.

His emerald-green eyes bore into me almost uncomfortably. It was like he could see right through me to the exact reason I was hanging out in the police station lobby.

A bubble of guilt rippled through me.

I shifted away from the wall and fidgeted with my keys. "I'm just waiting to have a word with my aunt."

He cocked a brow and tilted his head full of thick, black hair to the side. "And who might your aunt be? Maybe I can find her for you?"

"I just talked to her. She'll be back any minute."

He stared at me for a long moment, and I felt the urge to tell him to buzz off but held my tongue. He knew I was hiding something. I could see it in his expression. I wasn't normally a bad liar. Lying was a major part of my profession, but there was something about this man that caused my usually flawless lying ability to fly right out the nearest window.

"I'm Detective Tyler Black." He extended his hand.

"Barb Jackson." I shook the offered hand and simultaneously cringed as I recognized his name.

He frowned as recognition lit his eyes too.

"As in the Barb Jackson I spoke with earlier this morning regarding the Hatchett case?"

"That would be me," I admitted.

He frowned down at me. "First you call me asking to see the file, I tell you no, and then I just so happen to find you here at the station. Why do I have the feeling that you're up to no good?" He crossed his thick, brawny arms over his equally thick chest and continued to glare at me with those gorgeous eyes that I couldn't seem to tear my own gaze away from.

To be as sexy as this guy was, his attitude sucked. All right, maybe it wasn't his attitude that sucked. Maybe it was the simple fact that he was able to read me so well that I found so darned irritating.

"I assure you," I began in my best *I'm-not-lying* voice, "I'm not up to anything. I really am waiting to have a word with my aunt." Which wasn't exactly a lie. I was waiting for Aunt Mona. I just left out the part where she was gathering information for me on the down low that I'd already been denied access to.

"As you said earlier, there's nothing for me to see here regarding the case. Due to your unwillingness to share your information," I added with a hint of sarcasm, "I'll just have to gather my own evidence and prove my client innocent."

Detective Black smiled down at me. An arrogant, yet sizzling, smile that displayed a set of perfectly even, white teeth. "You really expect me to believe that you're here waiting for your aunt? You must think I'm as dumb as a rock."

"Not a rock. A hammer maybe, but not a rock," I said with a saccharine sweet smile.

He laughed, and for a split second, while his eyes were twinkling and his laughter echoed around us, I forgot why I was irritated with him.

I seriously needed to get my hormones under control before I did or said something I'd later regret.

"You're wasting your time with that client of yours." He air-quoted the word *client* with his fingers. "He's leading you on a wild-goose chase in hopes of throwing us off his tail."

"How would you know? You don't even know who my client is"

He shrugged his shoulders. "Jason King ring any bells?"

I blinked. "Excuse me?"

"Jason King. That's who your client is, isn't it?"

"How do you know that?"

Detective Black took a step closer to me, and I could smell his spicy aftershave.

Down, hormones, down!

"I'm a detective. It's my job to know these things."

I knew that it was childish, but I rolled my eyes. "Oh, please. Give me a break and cut the bull. How did you know that Jason is my client?"

He smiled a humorless smile. This man was dangerous with a capital D. I made a mental note to keep my eye on him.

"You said that you're working to prove your client innocent, and seeing as how Jason King is the only suspect in the case, he has to be your guy. That and the fact that you just told me." He grinned, and this time it reached his eyes.

Way to use your brain, Barb. I mentally smacked myself for asking such a dumb question. If I'd been thinking instead of gawking at the hunky detective I would've realized exactly how he knew who my client was.

What was the matter with me? I dealt with handsome men on a daily basis and never had any of them ever made me lose my head the way the good detective did.

I wasn't making a good impression as a private investigator. He looked at me like I was a rookie, and while in this case I was, I still didn't like it.

It wasn't my fault I'd never investigated a murder before now or been as irritated and attracted to a man at the same time in all of my life.

I wanted to smack him and kiss him at the same time. How was that possible? I didn't even know the arrogant fool.

Mona chose that moment to step out from behind the metal door and save my tail before I said or did something to make myself look like an even bigger fool than I already had. She spotted us, and her face paled a fraction before she recovered and made her way over to us.

"Hi, Barb. Sorry it took me so long, but it's been a bit busy in here today." She leaned over and kissed me on the cheek, then looked me directly in the eye. I took that as my cue to play along.

"I'm sure you know Detective Black." I motioned to the smirking mass of man in front of me.

Mona nodded. "Sure do. How are you, Detective?" she smiled.

I had to hand it to her. She was doing an excellent job of keeping her cool. She smiled up at Detective Black and patted his arm in that motherly way she had. I made a mental note to keep Mona in mind in case I ever needed an older woman to go undercover on a case. She looked like a pro. Adrenaline junkie that she was, Mona would end up wanting to make a career of it.

Detective Black smiled. "I'm fine, thanks. This is your niece?" He motioned toward me, an expression of disbelief creeping across his face.

"Barb here is my only niece," she said with a genuine smile. "We were supposed to go to lunch, but I can't get away. I hope it's no trouble," she said and turned back to me with a pointed look.

I understood exactly what she meant. She wasn't able to get her hands on the file, which wasn't a huge surprise. It was highly unlikely that the good detective would leave it lying around for just anyone to grab and have a peek at, especially after my call earlier.

"It's not a problem. Maybe later in the week." I carried on with her lie. "I'll let you get back to work and call you later."

She kissed my cheek, waved at the detective, and made her way back to her desk.

I looked at Detective Black and found him studying me from beneath a fringe of mile-long eyelashes.

"See. I wasn't lying," I said with a touch of annoyance.

Detective Black took another step toward me, and I pressed my back up against the cold wall. He pressed the palm of one hand against the wall above my head and leaned close to me. The smile never left his face.

"I'm not sure what kind of game you and your aunt are playing, but you need to be careful. This is a dangerous case, and that client of yours is no saint."

"Tell me about it," I mumbled.

"Come again?"

I shook my head. "Never mind." I didn't think telling him about my and Jason's rocky past was the best idea. That and it was my least favorite story to tell. I liked to compare my past with Jason to stabbing myself in the eye with an inch-long splinter I just spent an hour pulling from my foot.

He peered at me intensely. "I'm serious, Ms. Jackson." His expression sobered. "If you're going to go through with investigating for Jason King, you need to be careful. We wouldn't want to see you get hurt, now would we?"

It wasn't a threat or a warning to beware of him. He was simply warning me to watch after myself. I could tell from the softness of his voice and the expression on his face.

He let his gaze linger on mine for a moment longer. Then he turned on his heel and strode away.

The joke was on him. Jason had already hurt me years ago. But I understood the detective's meaning and wouldn't let his warning fall on deaf ears.

I watched his wide, retreating back as he waved at Mona then disappeared through the same heavy metal door I'd watched her make her way behind earlier.

My welcome was officially used up at the police station for the day, and I was in desperate need of caffeine, particularly in the form of an iced caramel macchiato.

I hurried out to my car, slid in the driver seat, and cranked up the air conditioning. My mind should've been going through all the things I could and needed to do to get this case rolling, but all I could seem to think about was the handsome, emerald-eyed, six-and- a-half-feet-tall, two-hundred-eighty-pound pain in the butt I'd just encountered.

My mind still raced as I stared off into the distance and asked myself, "What in the hell just happened?"

* * *

I hurried through the office door, drink carrier holding three iced caramel macchiatos in hand, and headed straight to my office.

Kelly spotted the coffee I carried and immediately followed like a baby duckling trailing after its mother.

I found Mandy behind my desk hard at work.

"How's it going?" I asked and sat the drink carrier on the desk. I handed Kelly and Mandy their coffee before removing mine and making my way around the desk to stand behind Mandy.

"Did you get to see any of the case file?" Mandy asked, then took an appreciative sip of her drink.

"No." I shook my head, shoved the straw in my cup, and told the girls about how Mona had tried to get the file. "Knowing Mona, I'm sure she'll keep trying," I said. "But I'm not expecting any success. The lead detective spotted me at the station and was on to me the minute he laid eyes on me."

"I see." Kelly spoke up. "Well, Mandy's been hard at work since the minute she walked through the door."

"What are you digging into first? Are you getting anywhere, and has it been easy?" I asked Mandy.

"Smooth as butter." Mandy grinned up at me. "I wasn't sure if you'd be able to see the case file or not, so I started working on the station's system, you know, just in case. Just one more minute and I'll be in."

"How long can we be in their system before they catch us?" I asked.

"Just a few minutes, five at the most I'd say, and I wouldn't risk printing anything. We'll have to be quick. Extremely quick."

I took a sip of my drink and allowed myself a moment to savor the smooth caramel flavor as it hit my tongue, then swallowed.

"Understood. Let's do this."

Kelly nodded her agreement from her seat across from the desk.

"And it's just. That. Easy."

Three final keystrokes and the police station's database popped up on my monitor. Mandy might be the one doing the hacking, but if anyone was taking the fall should we get caught, it would be me. I knew Mandy understood the risks of what she was doing, but there was no way I'd ever let one of my girls take the fall over a case I'd taken on.

"We're in. Now," Mandy flipped her long, curly auburn hair over her shoulder, "what exactly are we looking for?"

I leaned over her shoulder to get a better look at the screen and placed my palm on the desktop. "We need to see anything pertaining to the Lydia Hatchett case. Police reports, evidence, anything from the medical examiner. If they logged it, I want to see it."

I knew that our particular police usually kept two copies of all the reports. One hard copy and one digital. The police report would be public record, but the evidence and medical examiner's report weren't, and those were the reports I really wanted to get my hands on.

"No problem." She smiled and started typing. Moments later the screen changed, and she nodded. "This is the official police report. Of course, more could've been added to the hard copy of the file since this was logged in, and we won't be able to see it until it's added to this electronic file. So this report might not be complete."

"What does it say?" I asked as I fired up my iPad to take notes. I, unlike Kelly, understood technology.

"It states that Lydia Hatchett appears to have been murdered. No surprise there." She clicked around on the screen. "She was found facedown on her bedroom floor with a single gunshot wound to the back of the head." More clicking and scrolling. "There was no sign of forced entry, and the only fingerprints found at the scene belonged to the victim, her husband Robert, and Jason King."

"Not good considering Jason swears they weren't having bouncy-bouncy," Kelly piped up.

"Exactly." I made some notes. "Anything else against Jason evidence-wise?"

"Yeah." She clicked the mouse around. "They found a jacket and money clip that belonged to him hanging over the back of a chair in the bedroom where the body was discovered. Jason identified them as his, and his prints were all over them."

"He told me about those pieces of evidence when he came in this morning. Was a murder weapon found?"

Mandy scrolled down the screen then shook her head. "No. The medical examiner's report states that she was shot in the head with a nine-millimeter handgun, which was not recovered at the crime scene. The head wound is listed as the official cause of death. Ballistics is still pending."

"And Detective Black is the lead detective on this case?"

"Just a sec." She scrolled to the top of the page again and read. "Yes. Detective Tyler Black. Do you know him?"

I knew him all right. Since our meeting at the station earlier in the day I couldn't get the man out of my head, which was so completely uncharacteristic of me.

"Yes," I finally admitted. "I met him at the station this morning."

Mandy smiled over her shoulder at me. "You sound a little breathless there, boss. Is there something you're not telling us?"

I glanced up at Kelly and found her wiggling her eyebrows and biting her coffee straw with a smile.

"You two are hopeless." I chuckled.

I wanted to lie and tell them that the detective had had zero effect on me, but my ability to lie was nonexistent today, so I bit the bullet and told them the truth instead.

"Let's just say that he wasn't what I was expecting. He was...hot."

And remembering the tall, emerald-eyed, raven-haired detective, *hot* was putting it mildly. In all honesty, he was walking, talking sex in faded blue jeans, but I didn't have time for that right now, nor was I willing to tell the girls. They'd be playing *Love Connection* before I could finish the coffee I held in my hands.

Mandy laughed. "I see. Well"—she turned back to the computer screen—"what else do we need?"

I blinked away from my X-rated thoughts of the buff Detective Black and tapped my iPad.

"I need an address for the Hatchett residence. As much as I don't want to, I need to pay a visit to the crime scene. I know it's been two weeks since the murder, but the police might've missed something. Maybe Robert owns a gun that the police don't know about."

"An illegal gun?" Mandy asked. "We know the first thing they most likely did was run a search to see if Robert is a registered gun owner. Just let me get out of this system, we've been in too long, and the longer we're in, the bigger chance we have of getting caught. I'll get that address for you in just a second."

"Thanks," I said. "I'd like to do a little snooping. I also need you to do some digging into the background of Lydia and Robert Hatchett and our client, Jason King. I need everything you can come up with. Financials, properties they own, business deals and dealings, the works. Can you handle it?"

Mandy closed out of the police systems database and did some little move that cleared my computer of any evidence that she'd ever been snooping around in their files. She really was impressive. Thank goodness she used her powers for good instead of evil.

"Who do you think you're talking to?" she grinned over her slightly plump shoulder and hiked a thumb at herself. "I got this."

Her fingers flew across the keyboard, and seconds later I had the address to the Hatchett residence.

"Hold the place down until I get back. I'll check in when I get there."

Kelly tossed a salute at me. Mandy never looked up from the computer but called out, "Be careful."

I grabbed my purse and what was left of my coffee, passed through the office doors, and made my way out to my car.

Now, I know breaking and entering isn't the way every private eye does business, but it was the only choice I had if I wanted to get my hands on any overlooked physical evidence that might clear Jason of any wrongdoing, and to do that, I needed to search every possible avenue, including Hatchett's home.

Twenty minutes and one vanilla shake later (I know, not hip and thigh friendly, but I was hungry, and have you ever tried to eat a salad on the go?), I pulled up to the front of an enormous gated estate ready to do a little breaking and entering. After all, it wasn't like I could walk up to the door and announce that I was coming in to do a little snooping for the guy suspected of murder. And I wasn't as fortunate as the cops who could just wave their warrant in Hatchett's face then come in and snoop as they pleased.

Even if my approach was knocking on the front door, there was no one in the home to question. The Hatchett's didn't have any children, and I doubted I'd get anything out of the maids if they were even working on a Friday, which wasn't likely. Mr. Hatchett had probably demanded the household staff not speak to anyone about him or the murder anyway.

If there was an easier way to discover whether or not Robert Hatchett owned an illegal weapon, I couldn't think of it. Cheaters and liars are my specialty, potential murderers, not so much. As much as I hated to admit it, even to myself, as far as this case was concerned, I was winging it.

I steered my car to the side of the road and stopped. I pulled my purse from the passenger seat into my lap then rooted around inside until I found the slip of paper Mandy had written the address on and rechecked to make sure I had the correct address.

A quick scan of the neighborhood told me all was quiet. From the peeks I'd gotten of the neighbors' vehicles, Mercedes, Bentleys, and one very impressive Audi, my tiny red Volkswagen Beetle stuck out like a sore thumb.

I know. A red Volkswagen Beetle wasn't the most inconspicuous, sensible vehicle for someone in my profession, but I loved my car, and more importantly, it was in my price range. Cheap.

With a quick glance in the rearview mirror, I spotted a tall hedge on the corner of the Hatchett property. I put the car in gear, made a quick U-turn in the middle of the desolate street, and pulled up behind the bush. The hedge was tall enough to hide my car from prying eyes, so I killed the engine, grabbed my gun, a small(ish), very cute .380 handgun, and exited the car. I shoved the weapon in the back waistband of my jeans and pulled my simple blue T-shirt over the grip to conceal it, should I be seen.

As I stepped away from the car, my cell phone buzzed. I slowed my steps, pulled it out of my pocket, and read the display.

Kelly.

I pressed the phone to my ear. "Yeah?"

"Mandy says she just double-checked and confirmed that Hatchett does in fact have a meeting and should be out of the house for at least a couple of hours. You should be clear except for the staff, and considering that it's Friday, they may not even be in today. Mandy couldn't find a schedule for that, but you may not have much to worry about on that front."

"Excellent. I'm outside the gate about to head inside now. I'll call you in ten."

"Got it," she answered and then ended the call.

I put my cell on vibrate and shoved it back into my pocket. The midday sun glared down on me, and sweat started to slither down my back. I took a deep breath and quickened my steps down the sidewalk leading toward the backyard.

When I reached the rear corner of the tall, wrought-iron fence surrounding the house, I checked my surroundings. The rear of the Hatchett estate and the house across from it sat on the end of a dead-end street. Directly behind the houses was a slight hill leading up to a thick, tree-lined area. When I looked about and was certain I hadn't piqued the interest of any nosey neighbors, I stepped around the fence between the grassy hill and the back of the wrought-iron fence enclosing the backyard. Thick, green ivy covered the fence, giving the occupants in the backyard a semblance of privacy. I slid my hand between the vines and pulled them apart, making a gap just big enough to see through.

I pressed my face up to the opening and looked around.

The backyard appeared empty, so I switched my attention to the windows of the house. They too were void of life both upstairs and down. From the looks of it, I was in the clear where the household staff was concerned. I jumped as high as I could and grabbed hold of the top of the fence, hoisted myself up, and climbed to the top.

It took some effort, but I finally got myself into a position where I could slide my leg in between the sharp, decorative spikes lining the top of the fence. Once I'd finally wiggled my way into a sitting position between the spikes and steadied myself atop the fence, I wiggled both legs over to the other side. When I'd made it completely past the spikes and was on the other side of the fence, I dropped quickly down to the ground without incident. While crouched in my ninja position I took a moment to scan the area.

No alarms blared, and no ginormous dogs had me in their sights as their next meal. I was the only one in the yard. I sprinted across the yard just in case I'd missed someone in the house windows. Once on the amazing stone patio I slowed to a jog and then pressed my back against the wall of the house. I was in a secluded area but still worried that someone would see me, so I moved cautiously, back still pressed against the wall, toward the sliding glass doors.

I stepped over a small stone planter and leaned forward to chance a peek inside. From my vantage point I saw that the patio doors led into a well-equipped kitchen. Beyond the kitchen I could see the dining area, and even some of the living area and foyer were visible thanks to the house's open floor plan.

I didn't see any movement inside, so I slid my maxed-out credit card (thanks to my need for a house with food and running water) from my back pocket, just in case I needed to do a little lock-jimmy, but when I gripped the door handle and pulled, the door slid open easily on a set of well-greased tracks.

I released the breath I'd been holding. No alarms blared, which honestly surprised the business out of me. A murder had occurred in the residence only two weeks ago. I kind of thought the house would have a little better security, but apparently I was wrong.

Either Hatchett wasn't worried about a repeat performance because he was the killer, he hired the killer, or he just had no idea how lax his household staff was with security when he was away, because I could clearly see an alarm panel beside the main entry door.

I took a tentative step inside and slid the door shut behind me, thankful my shoes didn't squeak on the waxed-tile floor. I stood frozen in place and listened for any sign that I wasn't the only one in the house. When nothing but silence greeted me, I made my way across the state-of-the-art kitchen and into what appeared to be a formal dining room. From there, I tiptoed into a massive living area. The house was so quiet it gave me the heebie-jeebies, but I squashed the feeling, hiked up my big-girl panties, and located the staircase that led up to the second floor.

I figured it would be easier to search the upstairs portion of the house starting with the crime scene and work my way back downstairs. I learned in my training days that most people kept their safes in either the bedroom, home office, or study. I figured that if Hatchett owned a gun, he'd be smart enough to keep it in a safe.

Finding that safe, if it even existed, was my number one priority.

I quickly ascended the stairs and made my way down a long, wide hallway.

Most of the doors along the hallway stood open, so it was easy to see that the rooms were mostly guest bedrooms and bathrooms. When I came to the end of the corridor, the last door was shut tight.

I took another quick glance behind me, then leaned my ear against the door and listened.

Nothing.

I grasped the doorknob and twisted. Locked.

I grabbed my trusty old maxed-out credit card in between the door and the doorframe and began to wiggle it back and forth. What felt like a century later, I heard the telltale click of the lock disengaging.

With a sigh of relief, I cautiously stuck my head inside and peeked around.

Yeah, I knew this entire idea was a crazy move. I knew better than to be sneaking into the house of someone as powerful as Robert Hatchett where his wife had been murdered weeks earlier—and in broad daylight, no less—but what other choice did I have?

All right, so I had a few other options, but I wanted to get the case over and done with as quickly as possible, and the only way that was going to happen was if I put on my big-girl boots and took some outrageous chances.

It was my job as a PI to do the insane things no one else wanted to do in order to get the proof needed to clear my client.

I shoved the small trickle of fear of being caught back into its little box in the back of my mind, slipped inside the room, and locked the door behind me.

I glanced around the room and discovered that I was in the master bedroom. The room where Lydia had been murdered.

I stood still for a moment and took in my surroundings. The freaking room was as big as my tiny house.

The spacious area held a massive television, large four-poster bed, two nightstands, several bookcases holding everything ranging from books to DVDs, family pictures, and Fabergé eggs.

I'd always hated those ghastly eggs.

I spotted a door further along the room, most likely to a bathroom, and to my right I found another door that I assumed led to a closet. I hurried across the room and twisted the knob closest to me. Sure enough, it was a walk-in.

Boy was it a closet.

There wasn't an inch of free space. The racks were bursting with both men's and women's clothing, shoes, bags, accessories, hats, and much more.

This closet made mine look like the storage room in a Goodwill store. I was perfectly happy with broken-in jeans, vintage T-shirts, Converse tennis shoes, and a few dressy outfits for those occasions and undercover jobs that I couldn't get out of.

I stepped inside and did a slow spin in the center of the room. Strangely enough, I noticed that there were no boxes to rummage through. The drawer fronts were glass, and even I cringed at their tackiness. What kind of idiot would hide evidence of a murder in a glass-front anything? I felt around in the drawers anyway, just in case I was wrong. When I felt nothing but silky clothing and socks, I closed the drawers and stepped back out into the bedroom.

The room was so clean and orderly that one would never suspect a murder had taken place. No bloodstains on the carpet and no bullet holes riddled the walls. Not that I expected to walk in and see a chalk outline on the floor and crime-scene tape everywhere. It had been weeks since Lydia Hatchett was murdered, but I had to admit that I was a little let down. This being my first murder investigation, I suppose I was hoping for a little more, I don't know, excitement maybe?

The sound of my footsteps was absorbed by the plush wall-to-wall carpet as I found my way to the nightstand closest to the entrance.

I knew the chances of finding anything in the nightstands that would aid in my investigation would be slim to none, but I had to try. Sometimes the police missed things or passed them over thinking they were unimportant and had nothing to do with the case. I'm not saying cops are completely incompetent baboons. I mean, some are, but sometimes the smallest of items are overlooked and end up having the biggest impact on a case.

I pulled open the nightstand drawer and frowned. From the contents of the nightstand I was obviously on Robert's side of the bed. There was an old pair of reading glasses, one of his business cards, a roll of Tums, two expired condoms, lotion, a travel pack of tissues, and a DVD copy of *Busty MILF's IV*

I slid the drawer closed and quelled a shudder as an image of what Hatchett did with the drawer's contents crawled unwelcome through my mind. I shook away the gag-inducing image and made my way to the other side of the bed.

I knelt down in front of the second nightstand and pulled out the drawer. I was surprised to see little to nothing in this one as well. There was a tube of hand cream, a sleep mask, and a copy of *Reader's Digest*. I'd already decided that if there was a copy of *Burly DILF's IV* in this drawer, I was going to die.

I removed the items and shook out the magazine to make sure there weren't any notes tucked away inside, but nothing fell out.

I tossed the tube of hand cream back into the drawer and then paused when a hollow *bong* sounded. I picked up the tube again, dropped it into the drawer, and was once again met with the same hollow sound.

I snatched the cream from the drawer, tossed it onto the floor, and knocked against the bottom of the drawer in a straight line with the knuckle of my middle finger. Sure enough, when I reached the center of the drawer, the thumping became hollow. I slid my hand along the bottom until I reached the middle. I felt a faint line beneath my fingertips. With a little pressure, I pushed down. The panel popped out to reveal a shallow hidden cubby.

I tried to contain my excitement as I pulled the panel back. In the bottom of the hidden cubby were some small papers. As I pulled them out I realized they were slips from an ATM machine and a few receipts from a motel in Trinity Grove. Trinity Grove was a small summer town less than an hour outside the city. The amounts of the ATM receipts and the motel receipts were always the same.

I scrunched my brow. It looked like Lydia was fooling around, but with whom? Was Jason lying? I knew from experience that Jason lying wasn't a big leap, and I already suspected him of sleeping with her from the fingerprints in her bedroom. But I could only wonder, if his prints were in her bedroom, why would they be sneaking out to Trinity Grove to rent a motel room?

The receipts were a gold mine of evidence if I could figure out whom exactly Lydia was seeing at the motel. She was obviously doing something she wasn't supposed to be doing, and I was going to get to the bottom of what that something was. If she was seeing another man, it was entirely possible that he could be the killer.

I was busy shoving the receipts into the front pocket of my jeans to go over later when a black business card slid out from between two of the slips of paper and landed on the floor against my knee.

When I picked it up, my chin dropped.

It was Jason's business card, but what really held me in a stranglehold was the writing on the back.

In his bold script the message read:

I can't wait.

8:00 p.m.

Be ready.

Breath caught in my lungs. Jason *was* sleeping with her. The son of a beyotch had lied to me again. It was one thing for me to suspect him of lying, but it always burned me when I discovered that he actually was.

Would I never learn? I shoved the card and the receipts into my pocket, snapped the panel back into place, tossed the drawer's contents back inside, and slid the drawer back into the nightstand.

I stood and went in search of the gun safe. I looked under the bed and behind every painting but didn't have any luck locating the safe I assumed Hatchett had. Once I'd searched every inch of the bedroom and gotten all of the evidence out of the room that I was going to get, I decided that it was time to take a look around downstairs.

I'd just grabbed the doorknob when the faint sound of a door closing downstairs caught my attention.

I sent up a silent prayer that the door wouldn't squeak and twisted the knob. The door opened silently, and I tiptoed out into the hallway. Once outside the room, I pressed my back against the wall and slinked down the hallway until I could see over the railing to the lower floor.

As I leaned out to take a look at the entryway, I spotted a portly Hispanic woman waddling her way across the main entry with her arms full of brown paper grocery bags. She was headed straight for the kitchen, which just so happened to be my only exit.

If I made a break for the front door, I risked the chance of the maid catching me as I ran through the house, and there was no way I could make it out the way I came in, through the sliding glass door, without passing her in the kitchen and, again, being caught.

My investigation of the house was done for the day. I hadn't been able to check the downstairs for a gun safe, or hidden gun, and it was only a matter of minutes before I was found. This mission was over.

I doubled back to the master bedroom as quietly as I could and slipped back inside. I closed the door behind me and twisted the lock back into place. I scanned the room. How in the hell was I going to get out of this house?

Then I saw it.

Two long curtains covered what I originally thought to be another set of bay windows but was in fact a set of French doors. I rushed over and looked out. The doors led out to a balcony that overlooked the back yard.

I pushed through the curtains, opened the doors, and stepped out onto the balcony. Fortunately for me, the yard remained empty. Unfortunately, the balcony didn't have stairs leading down to the patio. It was a long drop, but if I could somehow distract the maid long enough, I could jump down to the patio and make a break for the fence. It would be quite a little drop to reach the ground below, but I had no other choice.

The only thing I needed to figure out now was how to distract the maid so I could make my big break. My mind raced. I pictured the layout of what I'd seen of the house in my mind, and an idea began to take shape. It was thin, and I doubted it would work, but I was out of choices.

I grabbed my cell phone from my back pocket and hit the speed dial for the office. Kelly answered on the third ring.

"How'd it go?" she asked.

"I'm trapped in the house," I said quickly. "One of the maids came in while I was in the bedroom, and now she's in the kitchen. I only have one way out of here. I need you to get the house number from Mandy and call. The maid will leave the kitchen to answer the phone, and then I can get the hell out of here."

"Got it," she said. "Give me one minute then haul tail."

The phone went dead. Moments later I heard the house phone ring. Three rings later it stopped. I assumed the maid had answered and took that as my cue to move it.

I slung one leg over the balcony rail, said a silent prayer to anyone who night be listening that I didn't break a leg on the landing, and leaped down to the patio.

Once my feet hit solid ground I took off at a dead run. I didn't spare a look behind me. I didn't have to know that I'd been spotted. The woman shrieking in angry Spanish was all the proof I needed. I reached the fence and started hoisting myself up between the iron spikes when someone grabbed my ankle.

I looked down and spotted the maid.

Who knew she could run that fast? I sure as hell didn't. She was barely five feet tall and shaped like a beach ball. I turned my head toward the street in an attempt to keep her from being able to identify my face should she be asked what I looked like by the cops she would undoubtedly call and at the same time tried to pull my foot free of her amazingly firm grasp without hurting her.

It wasn't until she started wailing on me with a frozen chicken that I let the whole don't-hurt-your-elders-or-innocents crap fly out of the window.

She'd nailed me again, this time in the shoulder, and pain radiated through my entire arm.

I pulled my knee as close to my chest as I possibly could with the plump woman dangling from my ankle and then kicked it back out. The force surprised my would-be captor, and she released my foot, tumbled to the ground, and rolled a few times. I would've celebrated shaking off Robo-Maid, but I didn't count on the force of the kick throwing me off balance as well.

I fell from the fence and cringed as the sidewalk rushed up to meet my face but was surprised when I was jerked to a sudden stop. The belt loop of my pants had caught onto one of the iron spikes I'd been sitting between. Before I could panic, a loud rip sounded, and a waft of fresh air blasted against my bare skin. I landed on the sidewalk with an audible thump.

Chancing a quick glance back, I spotted the entire back of my jeans and a scrap of my panties hanging from the top of the fence. Uncaring that I was now bare-assed, I grabbed my gun that had fallen to the ground, bolted to my feet, and sprinted toward my car. I yanked the door open, slid inside, and hightailed it out of the neighborhood before the cops came or, worse yet, someone saw my recently gym-deprived bottom flapping in the breeze.

CHAPTER THREE

———

I made the drive back to the office in less than fifteen minutes, which had to be a world record, but I was too freaked-out by my narrow escape to appreciate it.

My heart rate was almost back to normal as I came to a screeching halt beside the curb outside the office.

I killed the ignition, hopped out of the car, and ran through the glass door. Mandy and Kelly stared at me, both with wide-eyed expressions. I dove straight into my office and slammed the door behind me.

I pressed my back against the cool wood. Then and only then did I release the breath I'd been holding. The reality of how close I'd actually come to getting caught filled my mind.

Less than a minute later, it felt like the Incredible Hulk flung my door open. I slammed onto the floor, might've rolled a couple of times (thanks a lot Chips Ahoy!), and then came to a stop at the edge of my desk. I looked up at Kelly's stunned expression and flopped back onto the floor with a weary sigh.

"Crap! I'm sorry!" Kelly giggled then covered her grin with one hand.

"Are you all right?" Mandy asked with genuine concern from where she peeked over Kelly's shoulder.

"Do I look all right?"

"Considering the fact that you just ran through the office with your butt hanging out of what's left of your jeans? No." Kelly smirked.

Mandy hurried from the room.

It didn't escape my notice that she left out the part where I was lying in a heap on the floor because she'd just beat me down with my office door.

"Do you want to tell us what happened?"

As much as I wanted to forget what had just happened, I knew they would never let it go, and I needed to share the maybe-evidence I'd found with them.

Seeing no way around hiding the humiliating ordeal, I sat up slowly and hugged my knees into my chest. Mandy reappeared and held out a pair of black yoga pants and a cup of coffee.

"I had a spare pair in my bag. I was going to take a class after work." She smiled.

There were times when I didn't know how I'd survive without Mandy.

"Thanks," I said and took the offered items. Despite the fact that she was younger than Kelly and I, Mandy was like the mother hen of the office, always looking out for us, and for that I was eternally grateful. I just wasn't the maternal, take-care-of-others type. I loved my friends and was able to keep my cat alive, but let's face it—I could barely make instant coffee.

"Change pants, and then you can tell us what happened," Mandy said.

I didn't bother running to the restroom to change. Over the years we'd seen each other in the most compromising situations. Seeing my bum wasn't going to embarrass me any further or surprise them in the least. I shimmied out of what was left of my jeans and underwear, slipped on the yoga pants, and stood.

I made my way around my desk and flopped down into my comfy desk chair while Mandy and Kelly made themselves at home in the chairs across from my desk.

I took a deep breath and proceeded to spill the entire story, frozen chicken, rotund maid, and all. Needless to say, by the time I reached the end of the tale, they were both in uncontrollable fits of laughter.

"Only you, Barb," Kelly said between giggles. "I can see you hanging from that fence by the seat of your pants."

"I'm glad you think it's funny," I grumbled. "I almost got caught."

"But you didn't." She grinned.

"This time," I said.

"Did you find anything at all that could be of use?" Mandy asked.

I nodded. "Maybe. I was only in the house long enough to search the master bedroom, but I found something that might lead us in the direction of the real killer or at least in the direction of an affair." I reached beside me, pulled the receipts out of my discarded jeans pockets, and laid them out on the desk.

Both ladies leaned forward and picked up two slips of paper each.

"I thought Jason said he wasn't screwing the boss's wife." Kelly frowned.

"That's what he said," I answered, "but this certainly makes it look like he was lying, and if he's lying about this, I can't help but wonder what else he's lying about. I'm going to call him in. This case may be more trouble than it's worth if he's hiding more information from us. Or," I said as an afterthought, "she was having an affair with more than one man. Jason's fingerprints were found in her bedroom. If they were meeting up at her home, then why would they be sneaking out to Trinity Grove?"

"That's a good question," Mandy agreed. "It doesn't make sense."

Detective Black's warning to be careful flitted through my mind.

"Do you think he would go through the trouble of hiring you if he was really guilty?" Mandy asked. "I mean, what would the point be?"

"Detective Black seems to think that Jason hired us in an attempt to throw them off of his trail. He thinks that Jason is guilty but trying to make it look like he's innocent by hiring us. A *why-hire-a-private-investigator-if-he's-guilty* type of thing." I bit my bottom lip and shook my head. "Assuming Jason and Lydia were in fact having an affair, why would he lie to us about their relationship? He knew we'd figure it out when we started digging into the case." I tapped my desk. "I can see his reason for lying to the cops. I mean, they already have evidence against him, and adding the confirmation of an affair with the victim into the mix just adds fuel to the fire. But why lie to us when we're being paid to find the truth? I just don't get it."

"Me either," Kelly said quietly as she looked through the receipts. "Are you going to call him back in and ask him about all of this?"

"Not yet." I shook my head. "It's pretty much a lock that he and Lydia were sleeping together. I want to poke around some more and see what else I can find before I call Jason back in. If he's lying about the affair, then there's no telling what else he might be lying about." I tapped the pen against the desk. "Have you found anything interesting, Mandy?"

Mandy wiggled the green straw around in her cup. "No," she shook her head, "and digging into someone as popular and as powerful as Robert Hatchett, I fully expected to find something illegal, but he's as clean as a whistle." She shrugged. "If he's doing anything he isn't supposed to be, it's completely in cash and off the books."

"What about Lydia?" I asked, popping a piece of gum into my mouth. "Did you happen to find out anything on her?"

"Nothing. Absolutely nothing. All of their accounts were shared, and she didn't work. I did find some things out about her childhood though. Apparently she had a pretty rocky start. Alcoholic parents—and she was in and out of foster homes, which I guess would explain the nature of her charities."

"Had Lydia ever been in any kind of legal trouble?"

"Not that I could find," Mandy continued. "And again, I'm kind of surprised. Robert and Lydia dealt with so many powerful men and women, I thought surely over the years one of them would have become disgruntled over something, and some kind of complaint or something would come up, even if it was false, but I couldn't find anything."

"No out of the ordinary transactions that we can find, no employee complaints, and yet, someone kills the wife. Why?"

The three of us sat there staring off into space completely lost in our own thoughts.

"Am I interrupting something?" A deep voice yanked us back to reality.

"Geez! What's wrong with you sneaking up on people like that?" Kelly jumped up and blocked my desk from the man currently filling my office doorway.

I had the fleeting thought that my doorway had never looked better.

"I'll take that as a yes," he said. The hint of an amused smile curved his full lips.

I raked all of the receipts off the desktop and into the top drawer, then slammed it shut.

"Detective Black. What can I help you with?" I asked as I stood and instantly wanted to kick myself for how breathless my voice came out.

"Detective Black?" Mandy asked and raised her eyebrows in my direction.

I nodded in response. She immediately got my drift and smiled.

He was the last person I wanted to deal with at the moment, but there he was all swagger and charm staring at me with those enormous green eyes and rocking a body that could make a nun question her vows. If he was here, he knew I was up to something. He was too good a cop not to.

All I could do now was try my best to play it cool, and if all else failed, I could fall back on the good ol' deny, deny, deny, strategy.

He stepped around Kelly, who was doing her best to keep him from seeing me clear my desk, and crossed his arms over his chest.

"I have some calls to make," Mandy said and hurried from the room.

"You and I need to talk," he said to me. His deep voice rumbled off my office walls, and I suppressed a shiver. He was intimidating and sexy with his muscular build, chiseled jaw, shaggy black-as-night hair, and imposing stance. He was walking, talking temptation on a stick.

"Should I stay?" Kelly asked glancing between the cop and me.

"No, it's fine."

What could Kelly do? It wasn't like the detective was there to hurt me. Arrest me maybe but not hurt me.

She gave Detective Black one last frown and left the room.

Once the door closed behind her, I retook my seat and waved him to the chairs opposite me.

"What could you possibly need to talk to me about?" I asked.

"I think you know why I'm here."

"Umm, no." I shook my head.

Detective Black tilted his head back just a bit, lowered his eyelids a fraction, and glared at me.

I folded my arms over my chest and waited for him to say something. The tension between us was so thick I wondered if I would choke on it.

Finally he stepped forward and tossed something onto my desk, then took a seat in one of my office chairs.

I reached out and poked at the item he'd tossed down.

"What's this?" I asked in a voice I hoped sounded innocent but was afraid fell absurdly short.

"You don't know?" he asked succinctly.

I stared at the butt of my jeans splayed on my desk before me. I wanted to hide in a heap under my desk. Instead, I took a deep breath and shook my head.

I picked up the seat of my jeans and scrunched my nose. "Nope. Well," I corrected myself quickly, "it looks like part of someone's pants, but why would I know anything about them?"

He eyed me up and down. A chill slid the length of my spine. He was on to me. He knew exactly what I'd been up to. The scrap of my jeans and the fact that he was in my office was solid proof of that. From the expression on his face, he wasn't buying my innocent act at all, and who could blame him? I was falling disgustingly short in the acting-innocent department.

He knew I'd broken into Hatchett's place and was just baiting me along until I slipped up and spilled the beans.

That freaking maid.

Little did he know, I was as stubborn as they come.

"Weren't you wearing jeans earlier at the station?" He crossed his arms across his chest.

"I don't know, was I?" I pretended to have forgotten.

He cocked a brow at me like he wasn't buying a single word I said.

"And even if I was," I continued, "is it against the law for a woman to slip into some yoga pants on occasion?"

"It is if slipping into them comes after breaking into Robert Hatchett's place."

"I don't know what you're talking about."

"Oh, yes, you do." He smiled and leaned forward placing his elbows on his knees. "As a matter of fact, I have proof that you broke into his house."

"And what proof might that be?"

"I made a trip out to the Hatchett residence to ask a few more questions this afternoon. Imagine my surprise when I saw you running to your car then speeding away."

It took everything I had in me to keep my jaw from hitting the floor. Not only had the maid busted me but I'd been so wrapped up in my quick getaway that I'd completely missed a police officer watching from the sidelines? Why was I surprised that he'd caught me? He was a detective after all. Seeing me in the station had put me on his radar. All I could do now was deny, deny, deny and hope he let it go.

I pursed my lips and shook my head. "Sorry, you must've seen someone who looked a lot like me."

"And I suppose this someone drives the same car you do too?"

I nodded.

The vein in his neck looked like it was about to explode as he clenched his jaw, and for a moment I wondered if I'd gone too far.

"Let's cut the crap, Barb." The smile left his face. "I know all about your little fling with Jason King. I know that you were engaged." He leaned back in the chair. "I know he came to you early this morning to ask for your help, and I know that you broke into Hatchett's house a little more than an hour ago. What I don't know"—he scrubbed a finger along his chin and jaw—"is why on Earth you would jeopardize your life trying to help some lying scumbag like Jason King? He killed Lydia Hatchett, and it's only a matter of time before I prove it."

"How did you know Jason came by here? Have you been following my client?"

He smiled at me, displaying his perfectly even, white teeth.

"No, I wasn't following him, but after I saw you at the station this morning, I did a little more digging into his background. I did a little digging into yours as well." He pointed at me quickly. "That's when I discovered that the two of you used to be an item."

"And?"

"And it got me to wondering. What would you be willing to do for him?"

"You mean you started wondering if I would be willing to help him weasel his way out of a murder conviction," I stated heatedly.

"Something like that." He nodded. "The minute you introduced yourself in the station I knew that you were up to something. I knew you'd be sticking your nose where it doesn't belong." He drummed his fingers against his knee. "I already have some good evidence against Jason King, and it's only a matter of time before I can prove him guilty of murder, so if I were you, I'd drop this case, and let me do my job. Jason King is wasting your time."

The joke was on him. I knew exactly what evidence he had against Jason, and it wasn't enough to put him behind bars. There was no murder weapon, and if they were going on fingerprints alone then they'd have to arrest Robert Hatchett as well. He was just trying to scare me away from the case, but it wasn't going to work.

"Is that so?" I scoffed. "Well"—I shrugged with my palms up in the air—"if you know for a fact that I broke into Hatchett's place, why aren't you arresting me right now?" I asked.

He rubbed his palms against his thick thighs and smiled. "Let's just call it professional courtesy."

"Or lack of damming evidence," I rebutted.

"Oh, I have some pretty damning evidence against you." He chuckled. "Starting with the assless jeans lying next to your chair." He grinned. "You know, that evidence is out in the open. I could take it if I wanted to."

I glanced down at the offending item and bit my lip. If I wasn't busted before, I definitely was now.

"Imagine the look on my face when I saw you get knocked off of that fence with a frozen chicken." He started laughing. "And then your bare cheeks running down the street."

He'd seen my bare butt jiggling down the street. I was officially mortified. As soon as he left, I was hitting up a CrossFit class and dragging Kelly along for some semblance of moral support, even if she did just sit in the corner with a chocolate shake and watch.

I glared at Detective Black while he cleared his throat and regained some semblance of self-control. When he'd finally gotten his laughter contained, he asked, "Would you like to explain to me why you entered the Hatchett estate? Did King really hire you, or are you just doing your boyfriend a favor and covering his ass?"

My jaw dropped.

"First of all, Jason is not my boyfriend. We ended a long time ago, and that's a time in my life I'd rather leave forgotten."

Detective Black kept his gaze steadily trained on my face.

I tossed my hands in the air. "Do you really think I'm helping him get away with murder? Are you out of your ever-loving mind?"

Yeah, I was a little scatterbrained when the detective was around, but did he really think I was stupid enough to help someone cover up a murder?

I pulled a piece of gum out of my top desk drawer and set it in front of me on the desk.

"Jason King showed up this morning and asked me to help prove his innocence since you seem set to take him down without any real evidence. I do a lot of crazy things for my clients but helping them cover up a murder isn't one of them."

"How would you know what evidence I do or don't have against him?"

"I'm a private detective. It's my job. I have my ways."

We stared at each other, neither of us willing to budge on our stance for what felt like eternity.

He blew out a frustrated breath and shoved his hand through his inky black hair.

"Let's cut the bull, Barb." He relaxed in the chair. "We don't know each other that well, but the two times that our paths have crossed today you've been heading straight for trouble, and even though I don't know you, I still don't want to see you wind up hurt because of this guy."

"I'm not covering for Jason," I said adamantly.

He blew out a sigh and tapped his fist on his jean-clad knee. "I believe you."

I blinked uncertainly. "Did I just hear you correctly? Did you say that you believe me?"

He made a face at my sarcasm then nodded his head. "Yes, you heard correctly, but I do think he's dragging you into something that could get you in trouble or worse yet, hurt. He's not a good guy, Barb."

"You don't have to warn me about Jason. I already know." I shrugged. "Besides, I'm a grown woman. I can take care of myself."

I swear I heard him growl.

"You may be a grown woman, but you're also a fairly new PI. Just promise me that you'll watch your back. If you absolutely have to take on this case, be careful."

I appreciated his worry for my safety, but I also felt irritated because he thought I couldn't handle myself.

"Are you saying that because I've never taken on a murder case that I'm some kind of amateur? That I'm not just as good a detective as you are simply because I don't work for the police department?"

My blood pressure started to rise. I felt my face grow hot.

"No, that's not what I'm saying. I'm just warning you to be careful. Sometimes the person you think you know turns out to be a total stranger."

I took a deep breath, because whether I liked it or not, his warning was something Jason had taught me years ago. I'd thought I knew him, but I hadn't. Was Jason taking advantage of me by playing me again? Detective Black had given me something to think about.

"I was hired by Jason King to prove his innocence, and that's exactly what I'm going to do."

His brilliant green eyes glittered with warning. A prickle of heat skittered across my skin. He was as hot as sin in the summertime. His gaze bore into mine, and I had to grip the edge of my desk to keep from squirming. He was a big, sexy, pain in my butt, and I wanted nothing more than to throw him down on the desk and ride out my frustration.

It was totally the wrong thought to think at the time, but hey, my love life was practically nonexistent and had been for more than a year. Sexy stray thoughts were bound to buzz through my head from time to time, especially with someone like Detective Black breathing down my neck.

He stood abruptly and strode to my office door.

He turned back to face me. "I'm warning you," he said and pointed at me. "Be careful, and stay out of my way, because I won't hesitate to throw your butt in jail next time I catch you running half-naked down the street...no matter how beautiful you are."

CHAPTER FOUR

———

I would not let the fact that a hunky detective had called me beautiful interfere with my job.

My dreams maybe but not my job. After Detective Black left my office and I'd given Kelly and Mandy a rundown of Detective Black's visit, they'd called it a day. About an hour later I decided to follow their lead. It had been a long day, and I was starving. I powered down my computer, tossed the offending remnants of my jeans in the trashcan, locked up the office, and went home.

The second I walked into the house my cat, Mickey, twisted himself around my ankles begging for a pet and some food, even though his dish was almost completely full. Mickey was pretty demanding, but I chalked that up to the fact that he was a male. I'd never met a male anything that wasn't somewhat demanding.

I filled Mickey's dishes with fresh food and water, patted him on the head, and made my way to the shower.

As the hot water ran over my head and shoulders, I let myself run through what I knew about the case thus far.

The receipts to the motel in Trinity Grove were enough to tell me there was a big chance that Jason and Lydia were having an affair. Still, I couldn't shake the question of why Jason and Lydia would be sneaking out to the Grove when they'd obviously been meeting in Lydia's home. How else would Jason's fingerprints and personal items have gotten in her bedroom?

There was also the possibility that she was sleeping with someone other than Jason, and that's why she was sneaking out to the Grove. Wouldn't that serve Jason the Cheater right? His mistress cheating on him with a man other than her husband? I shook the malicious thought out of my mind and finished my shower, dried off, and slipped into bed.

Why was Detective Black so sure that Jason was guilty? Did he know something that I didn't? I'd seen the police report. There was nothing there that would suggest Jason actually killed Lydia. Finding a jacket and money clip was a far cry from finding a murder weapon.

One thing was for certain, Detective Black would be keeping tabs on me now that he knew I was serious about the case, and that wasn't a good thing for me. I'd have to be sneakier than usual to keep him from stopping or interfering with my investigation.

It was kind of sweet that he was worried about me, but that didn't change my mind about the case.

I wiggled down in the thick, fluffy linens and closed my eyes. Mickey hopped up on the bed and snuggled up against me. I put my arm around him, and with thoughts of detectives, murders, and affairs buzzing through my mind, finally fell asleep.

* * *

I'd intended to get some much-needed shut-eye, but all I ended up getting was some disturbingly sexy dreams of me rolling around with an extremely naked Detective Tyler Black.

I didn't know what my problem was, but I needed to get a grip. There was a murder to solve, and I'd get nowhere if I kept letting Detective Black wreak havoc on my mind. Launching my business into a different income bracket and freeing an innocent man teetered in the balance. I needed to get a grip and get down to business.

I felt a little bit like a zombie, so I hopped back into the shower in an attempt to wake myself up. Mickey stationed his perverted self right outside the glass shower door to watch the show.

Like I said before, I chalked it up to him being a male and let it go.

When the hot water ran out, I got out of the shower, dried, and tossed on a pair of comfortable jeans, a baby pink T-shirt, and a matching pair of Converse tennis shoes. My hair was a mess, as it always was in my eyes, so I ran my fingers with a little leave-in conditioner on them through it in an attempt to tame my naturally loose waves. When I no longer resembled a lion, I washed my hands and turned off the bathroom lights.

Mickey followed me through the house, so I checked his dishes, made sure there was plenty of fresh food and water in them, gave him a quick snuggle, then grabbed my purse, locked the door, and left the house.

The seasons were taking their sweet time changing, and the midmorning was already so hot, I was starting to sweat. I tossed my purse into the passenger seat and hopped into my car. I was ever so thankful for the air conditioner.

It's the little things, you know?

Once I'd backed out of the driveway, I headed toward the nearest coffee shop. Yes, I could've made coffee at my place, but like I said before, I wasn't great at the domestic things, even making the one thing I couldn't seem to live without. I really needed to at least learn to make a decent cup of coffee.

I turned off the main road and into the parking lot of my favorite coffee shop. I had a big day of investigating planned, and there was no way I was going to start I without my beloved coffee.

I pulled up to the drive-thru window and placed my order.

While I waited on my order to be filled, I checked my text messages and found that for once I didn't have any, so I switched over and checked my email. I had three messages waiting in my inbox. One from a disgruntled husband whom I'd busted two weeks ago, thanking me for ruining his marriage. I laughed because, honestly, I thought it was his cheating that ruined his marriage. The other two were potential clients asking for a meeting. Most of my clients came into the office or called, but I knew how embarrassing it could be to admit that someone could possibly be cheating on you, so I also offered to make appointments via email.

I forwarded the emails to Mandy so that she could set up the appointment, then closed out my email and tossed the phone into my purse.

The kind woman at the window handed my order to me and slid the window shut with a smile. I set the drink carrier in the passenger seat beside my purse and pulled back out into traffic. Ten minutes later I pulled up next to the curb outside the office.

I killed the ignition, grabbed my purse and the drink carrier, and got out of the car. I bumped the door shut with my hip and made my way across the sidewalk and into the office.

When I walked inside I found Kelly and Mandy behind their desks, already hard at work. I set a coffee on each of their desks and pulled up a chair.

"Rough night, boss?" Mandy smiled and pulled her cup closer to her.

"Something like that," I replied and took a refreshing sip of my own coffee. "Anything happen before I came in?"

"Nothing." Kelly shook her head. "To be honest, we just got in ourselves," Kelly said. "There're donuts on the desk if you're hungry." She pointed to a bright-pink box on the desktop.

"Thanks. You know me I'm always hungry," I said and grabbed a donut and napkin.

"I was fully expecting to see the good detective waiting at our front door because he decided to change his mind and haul you to jail," Mandy said as she tore off a piece of donut. "I mean, I honestly can't believe that he let you off with just a warning. He saw you hop the fence and everything for heaven's sake." Mandy shook her head.

"Believe me. No one was more surprised by that than me," I admitted with a shake of my head. "I just knew he was going to haul me in the minute he tossed the back of my pants on the desk. He said it was professional courtesy, but I think he took pity on me because I was assaulted with a frozen chicken and ran down the street with my bum hanging out for the entire neighborhood to see." I rolled my eyes.

"I think he likes you." Mandy nodded emphatically. "I heard him call you beautiful as he was leaving, and the way he looked at you..." Mandy fanned herself.

My eyes snapped up to meet her gaze. "Don't even go there."

Because I'd been going there in my dreams all night long. Enough was enough.

She smiled and shrugged but dropped the subject. Mandy was good at letting things go, unlike Kelly who held on for dear life.

"Do I have anything on the agenda for today?" I asked quickly, before Kelly had a chance to latch on to the subject of the detective and me. I pinched the bridge of my nose and closed my eyes.

"Your day's wide open, boss," Mandy answered. "I got those emails you forwarded me and called the clients. They're both on the books for next week."

"Thanks. Normally I'd celebrate the spare time and take us all out to lunch, but this Jason King case is top priority. I need to do a little questioning."

Kelly nodded. "Who do you plan to question first?"

"I thought I'd try to question Robert Hatchett. I probably won't get anywhere, but I have to at least try."

"The killer is usually the spouse," Kelly said and stirred the caramel that had settled in the bottom of her cup with her straw.

"I know, but from what I've gathered from the media and the police report, Robert has a solid alibi for the night his wife was murdered."

"And that would be?" Kelly asked.

"He was at a charity fundraiser. There're even pictures of him there with some of the models he represents."

"Why wasn't his wife with him?" Mandy wondered aloud.

I shrugged. "That's what I want to ask him. She's the one we see all over the media supporting their charitable organizations. Why would he be at the banquet when she wasn't?" I took a bite of my donut, chewed, and swallowed. "Besides, just because Robert didn't kill his wife with his own hands doesn't mean he didn't hire someone to do it for him."

The girls nodded their agreement.

"What excuse did Hatchett give the cops as to why his wife hadn't accompanied him?" Kelly asked.

I swallowed the last remnants of the coffee in my cup, then reached into my purse, pulled out a piece of gum, and popped it into my mouth. "Hatchett's statement said that he claimed his wife chose not to come with him to the banquet at the last minute because she wasn't feeling well, but I'm not buying it."

"Sounds fishy to me too," Kelly agreed.

"I want you to come with me," I said to Kelly. "I'm not expecting anything to go down, but I'd like a second set of eyes and ears just to make sure nothing slips past me.

"You got it." Kelly nodded. "When do we leave?"

"As soon as you're ready. We need to change into something a little more professional first. There're a couple outfits in my office closet." I stood and tossed my napkin in the trash. "I'd like to get this line of questioning over with. I really don't think Hatchett had his wife killed. I can't explain why. It's just a feeling I have. With those odd receipts I found in Lydia's nightstand, I think there's much more going on here than a disgruntled husband. I just can't put my finger on what that something is though. Not yet, anyway."

"Let's get changed, and then I'm ready when you are." Kelly tossed her cup in the trashcan and rubbed her hands together rapidly.

I turned to Mandy. "Can you hold down the office until we get back?"

"No problem, boss," she said with a smile. "But how do you plan on getting him to talk to you? His wife was just murdered. I'm sure the cops questioned him like crazy. Do you really think he's going to want to answer questions from a complete stranger?"

If there was one thing I'd learned about moguls like Robert Hatchett, it was that they loved the spotlight. After his wife's death, the media had been all over him. His name, business, and some of his clients had been all over the news, which meant more exposure for him and his company, which in turn meant the possibility of new clients, bigger contracts, and bigger money for Hatchett.

He might not talk to a couple of private investigators, but I was fairly certain he'd talk to a couple of reporters.

I tapped my bottom lip. "I'm thinking that he'll talk to a couple of reporters. If we say that we're doing a story on his charities, that might at least get us in his door. After that, we'll just have to wing it and get as much info as we can before he kicks us to the curb."

"What if he discovers who you are and who you're working for?"

I spat out my gum and took another donut from the box. (Don't judge me. My jeans still fit.)

"If Hatchett knows I'm working to clear Jason, he won't answer any questions I ask, that's for certain. But this is a risk we'll just have to take."

"What if he doesn't think Jason did it?" Mandy asked.

I paused with the donut midway to my mouth and stared at Mandy. "I never thought of that. But the cops have Jason's money clip and jacket as evidence. His fingerprints were all over the room. Surely that's convinced Hatchett that Jason killed her."

"That coupled with the fact that Jason doesn't have an alibi for the night of the murder, it looks more and more like he did it. I agree with Barb," Kelly said. "I don't think Hatchett will give us the time of day. But I also can't see why Jason would hire us if he was guilty."

I swallowed the last of my donut. "I don't know, but I think it's about time we find out."

* * *

Twenty minutes and Kelly giving three people the finger later, we found the Hatchett Modeling Agency. We got lucky and found a free parking space across the street.

The building was a tall, twelve-story, glass-and-chrome nightmare. The noonday sunlight reflected off the glass in a prism of color. I often wondered how the glare from the building hadn't caused any car accidents in the years since it had been constructed.

I checked my appearance in the rearview mirror and applied a fresh coat of lip gloss. While I wasn't a fashionista or diva by any stretch of the imagination, I still liked to look good and felt I could do so even without applying so much makeup that I had to use a putty knife to scrape it all off at the end of the day.

"All set," Kelly said as she pursed her lips in the compact mirror she held.

I nodded. "It's now or never."

Kelly snapped her compact shut and tossed it in her handbag.

Getting any useful information out of Robert Hatchett was a longshot, but I was determined to get him to talk to us. In all my short years as a private investigator, boobs, whether they were bare or covered and attached to a hot girl or not, and the promise of being in the spotlight usually got the job done.

We got out of my tiny red Beetle, locked the doors, and hurried across the semi-busy street while there was a slight lull in the traffic.

Kelly adjusted her skirt, and I fluffed my wavy hair one final time before we pushed through the revolving door that led into the main floor of the Hatchett Modeling Agency.

The interior décor matched the chrome and glass of the exterior. Even the main receptionist station was a completely garish, all-glass-and-chrome structure situated in the center of the lobby. I looked at the clear glass desk and wondered briefly how the receptionist was able to keep from flashing her undies at every person who passed through the doors.

The floors were a gleaming black reflective finish, and once again I wondered about the receptionist's panty-flashing problem. Or any woman who wore a skirt for that matter. I looked down to see if my panties were visible on the mirror-like floor but was surprised when all I saw was the swish of my silky black maxi skirt, everything else in the reflection was too distorted to make out.

Kelly and I made our way across the lobby and approached the reception desk. A six-foot-tall, blonde goddess who had to weigh less than a buck-o-five was screaming at the surprisingly calm receptionist about having to walk a block to reach the building because of the terrible parking. The receptionist handed her a slip of paper and smiled. The beautiful nightmare snatched the paper out of the receptionist's hand, tossed her hair over her shoulder, and stomped away from the desk toward the elevators.

The receptionist, a twenty-something redhead with a pert ski-slope nose and full, pouty lips, looked up and smiled at our approach.

"Welcome to Hatchett Modeling Agency. I'm Amanda. How may I help you?"

I was a little taken aback at her friendly demeanor but recovered quickly. I knew that this was a modeling agency, and she more than likely had to deal with divas and tantrum throwers, like the blonde who'd just laid into her, on a daily basis. Were it me in her position, I would've already tossed out some throat punches followed up with some eye gouges and been done with it.

"I'm Allison Reynolds, and this is my friend Kathrine Kelly," I lied, flashing the fake press passes I'd asked Mandy to whip up for us while we changed into more professional attire before we'd left, and hoped she didn't look too closely. "We're with the *Gazette*. We were hoping to have a word with Mr. Hatchett. We'd like to possibly do a feature on him and his wonderful charitable contributions."

Much to my surprise, she smiled and nodded her head. "Of course. Just let me make a call."

I stepped back and cast a sideways glance at Kelly. She shrugged.

"Mr. Hatchett would like to see you," Amanda said in a cheerful tone, then handed us two white slips of paper. "Take those elevators"—she pointed to the set of elevators to the right of us—"to the top floor and give those passes to the receptionist at the front desk."

"Thank you." I took the slips of paper from Amanda and handed one to Kelly.

Kelly's high heels clicked on the glossy floor as we took the passes and made our way to the elevators at a quick clip. Once on the elevator I hit the button for the top floor, and the doors slid shut. Kelly released a breath and shook her head. "That was a ton easier than I'd expected."

"I know." I nodded. "Let's just hope Hatchett himself is as easy to deal with."

"I don't count on it."

"Neither do I," I said reluctantly.

I'd never met a talent agent before, so I was a bit nervous with not knowing what to expect. I'd watched a few videos online of Robert Hatchett making speeches at some of his benefits and doing some interviews alongside some of his clients. He seemed like a cheerful, kind-hearted man, but that could all be, and most likely was, an act.

The elevator dinged when it reached our desired floor. We stepped through the doors and onto a floor identical to the lobby. The same clear glass desk loomed before us. The only difference between this floor and the previous one in the main lobby was the stern-faced receptionist behind the desk.

She wore a grey pantsuit (yes, I said pantsuit) with grey pumps. Her favorite color must have been grey, and even I knew better than to try to rock a pantsuit.

Her salt-and-pepper hair was twisted into a neat bun atop her head. She had a long, straight nose, thin lips pressed into a straight line, and her expression was completely unreadable. All in all, she looked like a totally ticked-off librarian.

Kelly and I shared a quick glance at each other but lifted our chins and made our way across the floor to the desk. We had questions that we needed answers to, and we'd be darned if we were going to let a grumpy receptionist keep us from getting them, even if she was a bit scary.

"I'm Allison Reynolds, and this is Kathrine Kelly," I said with much more enthusiasm than I felt. "We're from the *Gazette*. We're here to see Mr. Hatchett concerning a feature story we'd like to run." I repeated my earlier spiel to this woman and handed her our passes.

She looked over the slips of paper, looked up at me from over the top of her glasses, and raised one eyebrow. "I'm Carla," she said in a wispy voice. "Take a seat and Mr. Hatchett will be with you in a moment."

I thanked Carla, and we turned toward the waiting area.

Much to our surprise, the waiting area was fairly empty with the exception of two women, obviously models, or soon to be, relaxing on one of the plush couches.

We took a seat across from the ladies. I couldn't keep my foot from tapping as nerves slithered across my skin. I wanted answers and to get Jason out of my hair once and for all. He was a blast from the past that I'd rather never think about again. But now because of him I was in the middle of a murder investigation. One that put me directly in the crosshairs of a hunky detective who promised to lock me up if he caught me meddling in his business one more time.

In addition to getting Jason out of my hair and closing a huge career-making case, getting Detective Black off my back, even if closing the case didn't get him out of my head, would be a nice bonus.

A picture of Black getting me *on* my back flitted through my head, and I quickly squashed it. He was hot, intense, oozed sex appeal, and I was certainly interested, but I wasn't in the market for a demanding cop boyfriend at the moment, no matter how good the idea sounded in theory.

I was in the market to prove my client innocent and make an even bigger name for myself in my chosen profession.

"You shouldn't be nervous."

I looked up to find one of the women smiling at me. She was tall and rail thin with brilliant black hair, blue eyes, and exotically high cheekbones. In other words, she was gorgeous.

"I'm sorry? What do you mean?"

"Mr. Hatchett isn't like what you would expect an agent to be. He's really quite pleasant." She smiled kindly. "If he's agreed to meet with you it's a good sign. He usually doesn't meet with people unless he's interested in signing them."

"Thank you." I returned her smile. "But I'm not a model. We're reporters."

I actually wondered for a moment what kind of drugs Miss Model was on to have mistaken five-foot-tall curvy little me for a model.

"We're from the *Gazette*," I continued. "We're here to do a story on Mr. Hatchett, if he's interested." I motioned to Kelly and myself.

"Oh!" Her eyes lit up. "Is this about his wife?" She held her hand beside her pouty lips and faux whispered.

"Yes, it is," Kelly, seeing an opening to pump them for information, chimed in.

The woman nodded. "I'm Claudette, and this is Venetia." She indicated the woman seated beside her. "That whole mess with his wife was so sad for Mr. Hatchett."

"Really, it was," the woman introduced as Venetia said. "He was heartbroken." She pushed a lock of curly blonde hair away from her face, but it promptly fell back into place.

"Did you know Mrs. Hatchett?" I asked, jumping on the *pump-for-info boat* alongside Kelly.

"Not really," Claudette said and shrugged. "She sometimes showed up to speak to Robert when we were here, but she never really said anything to us. She was always smiling and very polite when she did though. She seemed like a pleasant woman."

"It was a bit of a shock when we heard the news of her murder." Claudette adjusted her blouse then looked back up at me. "I couldn't imagine anyone wanting her dead," she added. "She did so much for so many charities, it's just such a shock someone would kill her after all the good she did."

I nodded and tried to look sympathetic. "You said Mr. Hatchett took his wife's death pretty hard. How do you know that?"

"He didn't come in for a full week." Venetia's full lips slid down into a frown. "He cancelled all of his appointments, even put off a trip to the fashion shows in Paris. When he finally came back into the office a couple of days ago he just seemed so...*different*." She finished with a sigh.

"Different how?" I asked.

"Sad," Claudette answered. "He rarely smiles anymore, and that's quite odd. He's generally a happy-go-lucky person. Now, he says what needs to be said, listens to you, and then sends you on your way. No joking or laughing. Just all business. That's one reason we all love having him as our agent. He's so nice, and he makes us all so comfortable. Now, it's like he's a stranger."

I listened intently and took mental notes on every single thing the women had to say. There could be some hidden gem of information in what they said. I had no doubt Kelly was doing the same thing.

The question was, was Hatchett really that broken up over his wife's death, or was he simply suffering remorse over having had Lydia killed? It didn't really surprise me that these models were so quick to spill all they knew about the situation. After Jason hired me I actually turned on my television, something I rarely did, and the Hatchett murder was all anyone was talking about.

"Ms. Reynolds. Ms. Kelly. Mr. Hatchett will see you now."

"It was nice meeting you." I smiled and waved to Claudette and Venetia, then followed the stern-looking Carla down a long hallway. We stopped outside a pair of frosted, double glass doors.

Carla tapped on the door with her knuckles, then entered before being given permission. She held the door open and waved us through.

"You must be the reporters from the *Gazette*. I'm Robert Hatchett."

Surprised didn't cover the surprise surging through me at the sight of Robert Hatchett. I'd seen pictures of him online and on television, but he'd always been in a sitting position. The tiny man standing before me wasn't at all what I'd expected.

He was shorter than I, and I stood at only five feet tall. His light brown hair was thinning to the point that I could see the light reflecting off the bald spot on the top of his head (which I could also see easily). His nose was straight, his lips thin with a fine wispy mustache growing along the top one. His cheeks were sunken, whether naturally or because of his recent stress was hard to tell. I'm not exactly sure what I was expecting, but the tiny slip of a man standing in front of me wasn't it.

I quickly recovered from my initial shock and made our introductions, repeating most of the spiel we'd used on the receptionist to Mr. Hatchett.

"Of course. Please, please have a seat." He directed us to two plush leather chairs situated before his desk that made the chairs in my office look like those little plastic ones you find in a kindergarten classroom.

Mr. Hatchett retook his seat, unbuttoned his suit jacket, then placed his forearms on the desk, and regarded us with a smile.

"Carla tells me that you're here to do a story on my charities and charitable donations. I'm sorry I can't give you more than a few minutes today, but I have a full day of clients lined up." He leaned back in his chair and laced his fingers together over his thin middle.

"We understand that you're busy, so we won't take up much of your time," I began, "but first I'd like to say how sorry we are about your wife's passing."

A shadow of sadness passed over his expression.

"That must've been quite a shock," I added. "Losing her in such a manner, that is."

He glanced away, but when his eyes met mine again all I could see in their depths was grief. Genuine grief.

"Thank you." He cleared his throat. "She was a wonderful woman."

"That she was." I agreed, despite the fact that I'd never actually met her. "I understand she was the driving force behind the donations you've given and the many charities you've established?"

"Yes." He scratched his forehead quickly. "It was no secret that Lydia grew up in less-than-stellar conditions. She'd been in and out of several foster homes after her parents' deaths in a drunk-driving accident when she was eight, which is why most of the charities we've founded, and donated to, are children's charities."

All information Mandy had found already.

"Do the police have any leads? Any suspects?"

"Some." He frowned. His gaze grew shrewd as it began to bore into me.

"Had you or your wife had any problems recently? Any threats or people hassling you?" Kelly asked.

"You're asking a lot of questions about my wife's untimely passing," he said with a frown. "Would you like to tell me what any of this has to do with your story?" He looked back and forth between Kelly and me. "I thought you were here to talk about our charitable work, not my wife's murder."

"It doesn't have anything to do with the story," I jumped in before he threw us out on our rumps. "Ms. Kelly and I are just curious. From what we understand, your wife was well-liked, so naturally it's hard to understand why this happened to her."

He stared a hole through me, then leaned forward and placed his forearms on the edge of the desk.

He saw right though us. Through our cover, through everything.

"Let's cut the bull shall we, ladies?" he said. "Why are you really here, because it certainly isn't to discuss our charities. What do you want?"

I could've lied to him, but what good would it have done? He had us pegged no matter what I said.

I released a pent-up breath and sent up a silent prayer that he didn't throw us out on our ears before we got the answers we needed.

"Please, Mr. Hatchett. My name is Barb Jackson, and I'm a private investigator. This is my partner Kelly. I was hired by someone to find your wife's real killer."

"Does your client happen to be Jason King?"

I froze for a moment. It surprised me that he automatically jumped to that conclusion and asked with such a calm tone.

"I'm not at liberty to say," I hedged. "All I can say is that I want to find who killed your wife. Not just for my client but for you as well."

And I meant it. The man seated before me was a grief-stricken mess. Tears had swum in his eyes since the moment we'd mentioned his wife. I had a gut feeling that he had absolutely nothing to do with her demise.

He sighed and scrubbed his palm over his face.

"What do you want to know?"

I was momentarily speechless. I had expected some arguing, yelling, security to be called or something. Cooperation was the last thing I'd expected, and from the expression on Kelly's face, she felt the same way.

"Um, okay. Who do you think killed your wife?"

"I don't have a clue." He sighed wearily. "All I know is that I came home, and she was lying there, dead, on our bedroom floor." He sniffed. "That's a sight I'll never forget," he said sadly.

He looked so sad and forlorn that I had the overwhelming urge to put him up on my shoulders and buy him a balloon like any good auntie would.

"You mentioned Jason King. Why? Do you think he killed Lydia?" Kelly asked.

"Honestly?" He raised his eyebrows. "No. I don't think he did. The police said that he is a suspect, but what reason would he have to kill her? But then again, what would I know about it all?"

"What do you mean?" I asked.

"What I mean is, Lydia and I had been together for more than twenty years, and I'd never once suspected her of cheating on me up until the last couple of months. Then the police found Jason's jacket and money clip in the bedroom, but I'm sure you know that already."

I nodded, and he continued. "Why else would those items be in our bedroom if they weren't having an affair?"

Those were my thoughts exactly, but I didn't want to tell him that. He was in enough pain already. Confirming that I suspected his beloved deceased wife was a cheater wouldn't help the case any, so I let it slide.

"Had you had any problems with Jason in the past?"

"None." He sniffled and cleared his throat. "I hired him at the referral of a colleague, and he's been the model employee. His work is excellent, and he's quite friendly to everyone. I'm having a hard time believing that he's a suspect."

So was I.

"On the night that your wife was killed, you were at a charity dinner. Why didn't she accompany you?"

"She said she was sick with a migraine."

"Did you believe her?"

He shook his head. "I hate to say it, but no. She never had a migraine in all of her life. She'd acted odd all day, a bit standoffish, then about two hours before the event, she suddenly had a headache and told me to please go on without her." He shrugged. "At first I thought her odd behavior was due to her feeling poorly, but now looking back on it, I can only wonder if there was something else causing it."

"Did you notice your wife acting strangely anytime other than that night?"

He frowned, lost in thought for a few minutes, then scratched the side of his head.

"Actually, yes. About four or five months ago I was out of town on business. I was gone for two weeks. I called the house to talk to her one night, but our maid, Marta, said she was out with friends."

Marta. The chicken-slinger. My shoulder throbbed at the mere thought of that little, rotund woman.

"What's so odd about your wife going out with friends?"

"She was a homebody." He laughed. "She was one of those rare women who hated shopping and being in the spotlight. She spent most of her days reading, or in the basement using our in-home gym, or doing some kind of do-it-yourself home project, that sort of thing. When I called the next weekend I was told the same thing. I got suspicious, and when I finally got home I asked her about it."

"What did she say?" Kelly asked.

"She laughed and said she'd been spending time with some old friends she'd caught up with on Facebook. She said she was so excited to have met up with them again that she'd forgotten to call and tell me that she was going out. She said they'd been having some girls' nights out and late night chat sessions at the coffee shop and the like. I thought it was great. It always bothered me that she didn't have a lot of girlfriends, so I let it go. I was happy for her."

"Did you ever meet any of those friends?"

"No." He shook his head. "After she was killed I expected to see her friends at the funeral, but I knew everyone there. I started getting curious about them. When I got home later the night of her funeral, I searched for Lydia on Facebook, but she wasn't listed there. She didn't even have an account." He pressed a palm into the air. "With her lying about friends that didn't exist, and Jason King's money clip and jacket being found in our bedroom, I can't come up with any other explanation than she and Jason were indeed having an affair."

"I see." Poor guy. I knew exactly how he felt. Jason had cheated on me, and his wife had cheated on him with Jason.

Could Lydia have been meeting up with Jason while Robert was out of town and lying to her hubby about meeting with her imaginary friends to cover her affair? That was most likely the scenario, but I couldn't say as much until I had solid proof.

Robert was definitely on to something. Why create fake friends unless you were hiding something you shouldn't be doing?

I felt bad for the guy, which was a rarity for little ol' me.

My gut feelings had never steered me wrong in the past, and I was pretty sure this time wasn't an exception. I didn't harbor any doubts that Robert Hatchett was innocent. So the question remained. Who killed his wife, and why?

Had Jason gone off the deep end and killed her like Detective Black suspected?

No.

I couldn't bring myself to believe that option. Jason was a lying, cheating ass but not a murderer.

I stood and pulled my purse strap over my shoulder. "Thank you for being so cooperative, Mr. Hatchett. We really do appreciate all of your help."

Kelly followed my lead and stood beside me.

Hatchett pushed out his chair and came to his feet, then extended his hand.

"I don't know who killed your wife or why,"— I grasped his hand in mine—"but I'm going to do my best to find out."

He smiled a humorless smile that came nowhere near reaching his watery blue eyes and nodded. Then he released my hand and let his fall limply to his side.

"I hope you do. If there's anything else you might need, call me directly."

He fished in his pocket, pulled out a business card, and handed it to me. I slid the little white square into my purse and nodded.

"Thank you, again."

With a small wave, Kelly and I left the office.

We remained silent as we found our way back to the elevator. I hit the button for the lobby. I could tell there was something Kelly wanted to say, but we weren't alone. There was a woman, mid-to-late thirties, in the elevator with us.

We rode down to the lobby in thick silence and hustled across the main floor, then out the revolving doors. Once out on the sidewalk the heat of the afternoon sun slammed into us, and I felt the tiny bit of makeup I'd applied melting right off of my face.

We hurried across the street, slid into my little red Beetle, and I cranked up the air conditioner. The weather should be cooling off soon, and I couldn't wait for the season to change. I was an autumn kind of girl.

"You believe him, don't you?" Kelly said and tossed her handbag into the backseat.

I pulled my hair into a ponytail and secured it with an elastic tie I had around my wrist. The fresh air against the back of my neck felt like heaven on earth.

"Call me crazy but yeah. I do," I answered. "There's something about him. I just couldn't bring myself to picture him as a murderer."

"I agree," Kelly said. "But let's not forget. He is an agent. He plays hardball for his clients every day. That whole teary-eyed business up there all could've very well been an act."

She wasn't telling me anything I didn't already know. Even still, I didn't believe that Robert killed his wife.

"I know you're right, but I don't see it. I don't think he killed Lydia."

Kelly blew a tress of thick, black hair out of her eyes and nodded. "I was hoping you'd agree with me because to be perfectly honest with you, I can't see him killing a fly, much less his wife."

"So as far as I'm concerned, we can wipe Robert Hatchett off our list of suspects."

"We have a list?" Kelly asked, surprised.

"Well, no. Not really," I admitted. "Which means I need to get my rear in gear."

I pulled out into traffic and pointed the car in the direction of the office.

I replayed our conversation with Hatchett in my head as I wove in and out of traffic. I wanted to get back to the office as soon as I could. I needed to call Jason in and find out the truth about what was going on between him and Lydia Hatchett. I also needed to get a better look at the address on the receipts I'd found in Lydia's nightstand and pay that motel a visit.

I thought back to what little I knew about the town of Trinity Grove or the Grove, as people often referred to it.

It was about a forty-five minute drive from the city and was a small, yet booming, tourist town. That was about the extent of my knowledge of the Grove. Even as a child, I'd never vacationed there.

As much as I wanted to believe that this was simply a case of husband-kills-wife-over-affair, I knew that that wasn't the case. Robert Hatchett didn't kill Lydia. I felt it in every fiber of my being.

On the other hand, as much as I hated to admit it, even though I didn't think he killed Lydia, I did have some mixed feelings about Jason King and had ever since he stepped foot into my office.

"So, what's next?" Kelly leaned back in her seat and stared blankly out the windshield.

I glanced over at Kelly then back at the road.

"I need to pay a visit to the motel listed on the receipts and see if the owner or the night manager can tell me something. Like if they remember Lydia or Jason. Then in the morning I'll call Jason and have him come in. He's hiding something, and it's about time he tells me what that something is."

If Jason admitted to the affair with Lydia, but not meeting her out in Trinity Grove, his admission could be a lead in the case that I desperately needed. If they weren't meeting in the Grove then Lydia was meeting someone else, and that someone else could very well be the murderer we were looking for.

CHAPTER FIVE

———

When we reached the office after about fifteen minutes, Kelly's on-again, off-again boyfriend, Matt, was waiting to take her out to a late lunch. I told her to go and to have fun. There really was no reason for her to stick around. There weren't any clients scheduled for the rest of the day, and I could question the motel manager on my own.

Besides, who was I to deny on-again, off-again true (maybe, but not likely) love?

Mandy was on the phone when I entered the office, so I left her to her business and closed my office door behind me.

There were still a couple of hours left until closing time, so I settled in behind my desk and rummaged through the case file I'd put together. The file hadn't left my desk since I'd taken the case and was now full of financial records for the Hatchett's and Jason King, along with background information for Jason, Lydia, and Robert, along with the receipts I'd found in Lydia's bedroom.

I thought I'd have better luck talking to the motel's night manager seeing as all of the receipts were time-stamped after ten o'clock, which only solidified my suspicions that Lydia Hatchett was in fact having an affair. Why else meet at a motel late at night?

The question was, was she meeting with Jason, and if so, did something happen to give him a reason to kill her? I hated the fact that Detective Black had planted that question in my mind. Jason wasn't a killer. I knew it in my heart. He was a douchebag but not a killer.

I was leaning toward the idea of Lydia meeting another man who we had yet to discover. I just hoped that after paying a visit to the motel I'd be able to change that idea from suspicion to fact.

"Any luck?"

The door to my office opened. I looked up and pushed the hair out of my face as Mandy crossed the room and took a seat across from me.

She pushed a steaming cup of coffee across the desktop in front of me then sat back and took a sip of her own.

"Some." I stacked the papers and put them back in the file. "We found out that Lydia was well-liked among the few people she actually did talk to. Turns out she was a bit of a homebody."

"Really?"

"Yeah. Robert said she didn't really have friends and preferred being at home."

"Wow. I didn't expect that. In the pictures I've seen, she looked perfectly comfortable amongst all the people around her."

"Who knows? Maybe she was a good actor." I sighed and waved a palm in the air. "After we questioned Robert, I can't really bring myself to believe that he killed his wife."

"A nice guy?"

I nodded then rested my forehead in my palm. "The nicest, but not only that, he seemed...*genuine*. I have no doubt that he loved Lydia even though he suspected she might have been cheating on him. My gut is telling me that he didn't do it. Everything in me is telling me that he is completely innocent."

I picked up my mug and took a sip. "Thanks for the coffee, by the way."

She smiled and tilted her head as she took another sip.

I filled her in on the rest of what Robert Hatchett told us and how he'd acted.

Mandy leaned back in her seat and crossed her legs. Her black ballet flat dangled from the tip of her big toe.

"Is it possible that he was lying? Acting like the grieving husband to throw you off track? Like the way we suspect Lydia of acting comfortable around the people in the newspaper pictures?"

"Of course it's possible." I nibbled my bottom lip and thumbed through the mysterious motel receipts. "But I don't think that's the case. You should've heard Hatchett. How he talked about Lydia. I can't put my finger on why exactly, but I know that he's innocent. It's a feeling that I can't shake."

"And your gut instinct has never been wrong," Mandy mused. "So I guess the question remains. Who killed Lydia Hatchett and why? Do you think that there's a possibility that the detective is right and Jason hired you to throw off the cops?"

"Honestly?" I stacked up the receipts and secured them with a paperclip. "The thought has crossed my mind, but I can't bring myself to believe it. Jason has never been a violent man. A cheater? A liar? Certainly. But never violent," I said. "I'm hoping to get some answers tonight when I go out to Trinity Grove and try to speak to the motel's night manager." I held up the bundle of receipts and waggled them back and forth. "All of these receipts are from the same motel and are all time-stamped after ten o'clock. I figured I'd have a talk with the motel's night manager and see if they remember anyone fitting Jason or Lydia's description."

"Do you think Jason is lying? That he and Lydia were having an affair?"

"I don't have any solid evidence, but yes, I think so. All I know for certain is that Lydia was up to something, and I'm going to find out what that something was, if it got her killed, and whether or not Jason was involved. My hopes are that Lydia was meeting another man at the motel. That would give us another suspect to track down, because at this point, I've got bupkis."

I'd originally intended to wait until morning to talk to Jason about his and Lydia's relationship, but I needed some answers. Like were he and Lydia meeting out in the Grove?

"Before I head out to Trinity Grove tonight, I'm going to give Jason a call. I need to know for certain if he and Lydia were having an affair and whether or not he was meeting her out in the Grove."

Mandy nodded. "That would be good to know before you make the trip. If they were meeting at the motel, then there's no reason to talk to the night manager."

"Exactly." I nodded.

"Well, I have a few calls to return before closing time. I'll let you get back to business." Mandy stood. "Good luck." She smiled.

"Thanks." I smiled back at her as she left the room.

As soon as the door closed behind Mandy I grabbed my phone and dialed Jason's number. I needed honest answers from him in order for me get to the bottom of what Lydia was really doing out in the Grove and whether or not whatever it was she was up to could have possibly gotten her killed. I didn't want to hear him admit that he'd been lying to me. I really didn't want the embarrassment of going through that process again, but what could I do?

Someone knocked on my office door.

"Come in," I called as the phone continued to ring.

Jason walked in.

I disconnected the call and tossed the cell phone onto my desk.

"I was just trying to call you."

"I know. I was already walking into your office, so I didn't answer. Your girl waved me to go on to your office. She was on the phone." He smiled.

"Mandy knew that I needed to speak to you," I said. "What are you doing here?"

"I was heading home from the office and saw that you were still here. I thought I'd stop by and see how far you've gotten on my case. Have you found anything that could help?"

"Well, that all depends on how you answer my questions," I admitted. "There're a few things that we need to discuss. Have a seat."

I pointed to the office chairs, then stood and made my way to the side table and the full coffeepot waiting there. This discussion definitely called for coffee. To be perfectly honest, my entire life up to this point called for coffee.

Jason took a seat. His expression was one of worry and curiosity.

Despite our bumpy past, I had to admit that he was still as handsome as ever. His blond hair wasn't as immaculately combed as usual, and was slightly shaggy instead of his usual close-cropped cut. He wore jeans and a T-shirt instead of his usual business suit. He appeared much more relaxed. He'd changed some, but I wasn't dumb enough to believe he'd changed much.

I turned back to him and handed him a cup of coffee. I knew exactly how he took it. Two creams, one sugar. He smiled and took the mug, sipped, and then rested it against his knee.

I wasn't sure how to start the conversation off, so I figured I'd approach it like a Band-Aid.

Rip it off quick.

"I'm just going to cut right to it." I settled back into my chair. "I know that you and Lydia were having an affair."

He had the audacity to look ashamed and stare down at the floor.

"You lied to me...again."

In all honesty, I didn't have a single, solid piece of evidence that proved whether or not Jason and Lydia Hatchett were having an affair, but Jason didn't know that. The idea was for him to tell on himself.

And he did with his expression alone.

"I should've known you'd find out." He threaded his fingers through his longer-than-usual hair. "Look, it just happened. I wanted to tell you the truth when I first came to see you about taking the case, but I was afraid if I told you I was sleeping with her you'd refuse to take my case, and that wasn't a risk I could take. I need all the help that I can get right now. It's just a matter of time before the cops arrest me."

I could see where he was coming from. He was desperate, but that didn't negate the fact that he'd lied to me. If he'd lied to me about something as pertinent as his affair with Lydia, what else would he lie to me about?

"I'm not even going to say what I'm thinking. I don't have time for it right now, Jason."

He tapped his knee with the knuckles of one fist. "I'll answer anything you ask. Just don't drop my case," he pleaded.

"Then stop screwing around, and tell me the truth for once in your miserable little life," I snapped with irritation. "How long had you and Lydia been seeing each other before she was killed?"

He leaned back in his chair and blew out a breath. "A while. She came on to me one night after one of her charity events about six months ago. Robert had been out of the country with some of his clients on business. We'd been seeing each other on and off ever since."

I stirred my coffee with a skinny straw.

"Did she ever talk to you about wanting to leave Robert?"

"No." He shook his head. "She made it perfectly clear that I was simply a side piece, and when she decided it was over, it would be over. No strings attached. No attachments, period."

"And you were okay with that?" I asked skeptically. I found it hard to believe that he would be. The Jason I knew liked to call the shots. Most men would have a problem with a woman setting all of the ground rules in the relationship or affair.

"I was fine with it." He waved a hand in the air. "Now, if you're asking whether or not I had feelings for Lydia"—he leaned forward slightly—"then the honest answer is yes, I did, and I know that she had real feelings for me in the end." He looked me in the eyes. "But I'm not looking to settle down right now, and she had no desire to leave her husband. We were happy with the way our relationship was set up. I knew the scandal that would ensue should Lydia leave Robert for me. My career comes first right now. I had no desire to jeopardize it. I know that it sounds crazy, but that's just the way things were."

"And you don't consider sleeping with the boss's wife a danger to your career?" I asked in a disbelieving tone.

Call me crazy, but I thought having an affair with your boss's wife was a huge career risk.

"No. Neither Robert nor Lydia would have said anything about the affair because it would've harmed their reputations. Their charities and businesses would have suffered under the scandal, which means my career would suffer, and none of us would want that."

I understood what he was talking about. Keep your dirt hidden, and everyone thinks you're still clean, and the money keeps rolling in.

"Did Lydia ever talk to you about any old or new friends she'd recently reconnected with?"

He raised an eyebrow. "I didn't know her to have friends at all. She was a solitary woman. I can't see her having lunch dates with the girls. She talked to people connected to her charities, but I wouldn't consider them her friends. Their conversations were always business related as far as I know."

"Did you two ever meet out in Trinity Grove?"

He looked at me quizzically. "Trinity Grove? Why would we meet in Trinity Grove?" He sat forward in his seat.

"You tell me," I said and took a sip of my coffee, hoping he'd spill more details the way he spilled about the affair, but his expression remained puzzled.

"We met at her home or at my place when Robert was out of town, and we hooked up a few times in my office, but we never met in Trinity Grove. Why are you asking?"

He was telling the truth. It was obvious that he was now just as curious as I was about what Lydia had been up to.

I didn't want to mention the receipts I'd found in her bedroom just yet, so I played it cool. "I got a tip that she might've been spending some time out there. She never mentioned spending any time in the Grove?"

He frowned. "No. There's no reason she would want to. She was a city girl. Trinity Grove is a small town. I can't imagine her ever wanting to spend time out there. That's just not the Lydia I knew."

This new information helped me more than Jason knew. So far, I'd learned that Lydia was hiding her movements in the Grove from everyone, including Jason, for reasons I couldn't yet fathom. She wasn't meeting him at the motel, which meant that there was someone else out there who could've killed her. I just needed to figure out who that person was.

"Why should I believe anything you've told me?" I asked. "You lied to me yesterday when you hired me."

"Because." He sighed. "I didn't kill Lydia. I cared deeply for her. Look at me, and tell me that you think I'm really capable of killing someone, and I'll walk out of here and never bother you again."

I stared at him for a long hard minute. As ticked as I was at him for lying to me about the affair, I couldn't for one hot second bring myself to believe that he killed Lydia.

"I don't think you killed her," I admitted and blew out a weary sigh. "But if you lie to me again, I will drop this case."

"Understood," he said quickly. "I'm sorry to cut this short, but I have to get going." He stood.

I followed him to my office door. He opened it and stepped outside, then turned back and faced me.

"Listen, Barb. I know things between us went south, and I screwed up. I did you wrong, I know that, but I still think of you as my friend, even if you don't feel the same way about me." He scrubbed a hand over his face. "I don't want to go to jail for a murder that I didn't commit. I cared for Lydia, but if you want to drop the case, I understand."

Jason was a lot of things, but he wasn't a murderer. He was wicked smart. He had a heart, and he always started out with the best of intentions. But he also had a penis, and that's the part he listened to the most. That's what always seemed to lead to his bad decisions, but I couldn't see it leading him to murder.

To the clinic for a shot of penicillin? Yes.

To murder? No.

I stared at him for a few seconds, trying to figure out where the real Jason King had run off to, and who this person standing before me was. Maybe Jason had changed more than I'd thought? Yeah, right. Who was I kidding? But I did appreciate his apology.

I smoothed my hands down the legs of my pants. "Have you ever known me to be a quitter?" I asked and smiled. "I'll find out who killed Lydia. Don't worry about me." I propped my hands on my hips. "I'm a big girl."

Jason smiled, leaned in, cupped the back of my neck, and kissed me on the forehead the way he always had. "Thanks, Barb."

"Don't thank me yet."

I followed him to the main entrance and watched as he let himself out, got into his car, and pulled away from the curb.

I stood on the sidewalk as Jason's car disappeared around a corner. Night was falling, and the street wasn't as busy as it had been. The streetlights were coming on, and several *Open* signs in the windows of businesses across the street were now switched to *Closed*. Many people were getting into their cars and calling it a day. I wanted to do the same, but I still had work to do.

I was about to turn back and enter the office when something caught my eye. I discreetly scanned the sidewalk across the street from me until my eyes landed on what had caught my attention.

At the far end of the street stood a man. He was tall, dressed in all black. From a distance, he appeared muscular and had dark hair. He was far enough away that I couldn't see his face clearly, but one thing was for certain, he was staring directly at me.

I played it cool and calmly stepped back inside the office, but that's where my cool ran out. I ran past Mandy to my office and grabbed my gun. I slid it into the back of my jeans and ran back out the main door and onto the sidewalk.

I had no idea who I was chasing or why I was chasing them, but the way the mystery man was staring at me, I knew he was up to no good.

Did he have something to do with the case, or was I just jumping to conclusions? Was I being paranoid? No. I didn't think so. There was something about the guy that I just couldn't put my finger on.

I took a deep, calming breath.

I scanned the street again but was too late.

The mystery man was gone.

* * *

Mandy and I closed up shop around nine o'clock.

I watched as she got into her car and pulled away, then disappeared out of sight. The memory of the mystery man was still fresh in my mind. Who was he, and why was he watching me? Or was he even watching me at all?

Tossing my purse into the passenger seat, I hopped in my car, keyed the address for the motel into Google Maps on my phone, and pulled away from the curb. I hoped the cell phone would keep a signal until I reached my destination. I needed to break down and purchase a real GPS for my car, but at the moment the cost of one was out of my price range.

The Trinity Grove Motel was at least a forty-five minute drive from the office, so I cranked up the tunes and relaxed back into my seat as the city drifted by.

The lights of the city glittered in a rainbow of assorted colors across the windshield of my bright-red Beetle as I made my way out of town.

I cranked up the radio, sang along with the Rolling Stones, and let the events of the day roll uninterrupted through my mind. That mystery man had me unable to think about much of anything else. If only I'd been able to get closer to him. To get a better look at him.

I needed to let it go. As far as I knew, that guy was just another citizen making his way home.

Thirty minutes after I left the city, I entered the much smaller town of Trinity Grove. I'd decided to Google the little town and found what I read to be quite charming.

Trinity Grove, or the Grove, as it was often referred to, was a small lakeside summer town where many people from the city and surrounding areas escaped the hustle and bustle of big-city life for some rest, relaxation, and homemade apple pie. The Grove was best known for its down-home feel, lakefront vacation cabins, campgrounds, and summer Apple Pie Festival.

Living so close, I should've known more about the Grove, but I didn't. I'd just never had the desire to pay the place a visit. I wasn't a camp-in-the-heat-and-be-eaten-by-mosquitos kind of girl. I'm more of the sit-in-my-room-and-read type.

As I crept down the main street I passed a convenience store, a flower shop, several roads I assumed led to lakeside cottages, and a small mom-and-pop grocery store/farmers' market. The town, or what I could see of it in the dark with only the dim streetlights overhead lighting my way, would probably appear much more welcoming during the daylight hours.

But right now, the quiet stillness gave it a *Friday the Thirteenth* movie type of feel and was seriously starting to creep me out.

I shook the image of Jason Voorhees jumping out and whacking me with a machete from my mind. I breathed a sigh of relief when the robotic voice came from my phone and told me that my destination was two blocks ahead on the left.

I turned into the parking lot of the Trinity Grove Motel, found a parking spot, and shut off the ignition.

While I stayed in my car for a few minutes and tried to get my bearings, I observed the completely non-threatening structure laid out before me.

The motel was a bright, cheery sunshine yellow with sky-blue trim. The office was surrounded with a thick wooden porch that sported a large *Welcome to Trinity Grove* greeting sign. Brightly colored yellow, blue, and pink flowers flanked the stairs leading up to the office porch and along part of the motel's sidewalk.

I couldn't shake the feeling that I was in the wrong place, so I reached into my purse and pulled out a receipt to check the address. The motel was so cheerful in appearance that I couldn't imagine anyone having a sordid affair beneath its roof.

I checked the receipt. Nope. I was in the right place alright.

If Lydia was having an affair with someone other than Jason, would she go through the trouble of leaving town to rent a motel room, especially one this...cheerful? There were countless hotels and motels in the city. Why come all this way?

Then again, I'd seen men and women walk next door and pounce on their neighbor sunbathing on the patio while their significant other took a nap barely one hundred yards away, so I supposed this motel really wasn't that strange of a meeting place for an affair.

But still, why leave town?

The parking lot was more than half full of cars, which didn't surprise me at all. From the information I'd found on the Trinity Grove website, although summer was winding down, families were still flocking to the cottages and the lake beyond to relax and cool down for the remainder of the season. Those who couldn't get a cabin stayed at the motel until one opened up, or they found a place to set up camp by the lake.

I stepped out of the car and climbed the five steps leading up to the office door.

A small bell jangled overhead as I entered, and I was greeted with sunny yellow walls and sky-blue trim that matched the exterior. The rubber soles of my tennis shoes squeaked against the tile floor as I approached the check-in desk. I reached to ring the service bell, but before I had the chance a portly woman of about sixty (and I'm being kind here) met me on the other side of the counter. Her eyes were the same shade of blue as the room's trim, and her hair sat in a halo of tight, salt-and-pepper curls atop her head.

Her pink flowered muumuu was a fashion statement all its own.

"Welcome to Trinity Grove. I'm Melba. Are you checking in?" she asked in a voice that sounded like she'd smoked two packs a day since she was twelve.

I decided to take the direct approach. I hadn't been getting much sleep, and I wanted to at least try for a few hours tonight, which meant getting home before dawn.

"This is a lovely motel that you have here, but no, I'm not checking in. My name is Barb Jackson, and I'm a private investigator with Jackson Investigations."

"A private eye? Lordy, what's happened that a private eye has to come all the way out here?" she said with a strong southern accent that I suspected was as fake as her mile-long, ruby-red fingernails.

She fanned herself with her hand, and those same fake nails glinted in the overhead light.

I had the image of an ancient, plump, cigarette-stained Scarlet O'Hara flit through my mind and did my best to suppress a shudder.

"I'm looking into the death of Lydia Hatchett," I said. "She was murdered about two weeks ago in her home in the city."

"I heard about that on the news. Sad stuff that was." She shook her head and looked the proper amount distressed, but it seemed so rehearsed. Stiff, as though she'd practiced the speech in the mirror a dozen times before.

I immediately didn't trust her. There was something about Melba the Night Manager that set me on edge.

She was fake, but I decided to play along just to see what she had to say.

"Yes, very sad. What's even sadder is that the police may be accusing the wrong person of her murder."

"Why, that's terrible." She pressed her hand to her chest. What a drama queen. I fought against rolling my eyes. I nodded. "But I have reason to believe you can help."

"Me? What on earth can I do?"

"Motel receipts were found that put Lydia Hatchett right here at your motel at least once a week over the past few months."

"No, that's not possible. I would certainly remember her."

"Are you sure?" I pressed. I reached into my purse and pulled out a small picture of Lydia that Mandy had printed out along with one of the receipts that I'd nabbed from Lydia's nightstand and held them up to show them to her.

"You see?" I slid the receipt across the counter toward her and pointed to the address along the top of the paper. "This receipt is proof that Lydia Hatchett was, in fact, here. The room was paid for with cash. Take a look at the pic and think about it again."

The aloof expression Melba wore quickly became guarded as she peered at the picture and motel receipt.

"N-now that you mention it," she stuttered. "I recognize her. Her hair was different when she came in here, I think. That must be what threw me off.

Sure. Whatever you say, geriatric Scarlet.

"Mm-hmm. How often did she come in, and was she alone when she did?"

Melba hesitated a second then sighed. "She was always alone. She'd come in once a week, sometimes more."

Now that I'd provided proof that I knew about Lydia visiting the motel, Melba was a veritable fountain of information.

"How long did she stay during those visits?"

Melba bit her lip. "She'd rent the rooms for anywhere from one to three nights."

"Rooms? You mean she rented more than one at a time?"

Why would she need to rent out more than one room?

Melba looked like she'd just swallowed an entire lemon but nodded her head anyway. "Yes. Sometimes she'd rent three rooms. All kings. Never doubles unless that's all we had available."

"That didn't strike you as odd?" I asked. This certainly didn't fit the criteria of your average run-of-the-mill affair. Why would Lydia rent out more than one room? What was she doing?

"It wasn't my business, so I never asked." Melba sniffed indelicately.

"Did you ever notice anyone coming or going from those rooms except Mrs. Hatchett?"

"No," she answered a little too quickly. "I don't watch the customers coming and going. What they do in those rooms is none of my business."

"That's understandable," I agreed. "When was the last time she came in?"

"About two months ago."

"Two months?"

Melba nodded. "She said she enjoyed our rooms, but it was time to move on to a cabin. I saw her talking to Melvin Harris in the parking lot the last night she was here."

"Who's Melvin Harris?" I asked.

Melba waved a hand toward the front window. "He's a contractor who owns a bunch of cabins out on the lake. He's always selling existing cabins or building new ones to out-of-towners to use as their summer homes."

"Do you happen to know if he had any cabins available at the time he talked to her?"

Melba's frown deepened, and I knew I'd just about worn out my welcome. She huffed. "I only know of one that was still empty at the time, but I'm not sure she'd have been interested in it."

"Why is that?"

"It sits a lot farther back along the lake than the other cottages. The place is nice, but it's not exactly lakefront, which is what everyone is looking for. You have to walk a little ways to get to the lake from the cabin."

"Do you have a number for Mr. Harris available?" I looked on the counter for a stack of business cards but didn't see any. If this Melvin Harris built cabins, one would think he'd be advertising to the tourists, but then again maybe Melba didn't allow his business cards in the motel to keep from losing business when tourists decided to buy or rent his cabins instead of staying at the motel.

She narrowed her eyes at me then reached under the counter and pulled out a mammoth purse. She plopped it down on the countertop and fished around inside for a few minutes. "I'm sorry, but I must've misplaced it."

I wanted to call bullfunky but controlled myself. She was hiding something. I just didn't know what.

"No matter," I said with a big, toothy smile. "I'm a private investigator. Finding information about people is what I do."

Her already-sour expression darkened even further.

The bell above the door jangled, and the sounds of footsteps and whining kids sounded behind me, signaling that it was time for me to go.

"Thanks for your help. If you can think of anything else, please give me a call." I slid my business card across the counter. Melba picked it up and shoved it into her bag. I didn't expect to hear from her again. I was actually surprised that I'd gotten as much out of her as I had.

I skirted past a set of parents and their three wiggling, squealing kids and hurried through the well-lit parking lot to my car. As soon as I started the ignition, I pulled out of the motel parking lot with zeal.

I didn't get the answers I'd wanted. Instead, I'd walked away with a buttload more questions than when I'd started. Lydia Hatchett was shaping up to be a mystery all her own.

Why in the heck had Lydia rented more than one room at a time, and why so frequently? Why, all of a sudden, was she interested in buying a cabin? Jason said she was a city girl. Buying a cabin definitely wasn't like her if he was telling the truth.

The only reason I could come up with as to why she was out in the Grove was maybe she was afraid if she did whatever she was up to in the city, someone would recognize her or become suspicious of her actions, but again, what was she doing to cause suspicion? Taking out more than one room was something more than a simple affair.

I sped through the darkness down the road back toward the city with a million new questions rolling through my mind.

But the big question was, would I find the answers in time to save Jason?

* * *

I had gotten very little sleep and was up at the butt crack of dawn. The case was weighing heavily on my mind. Lydia Hatchett was turning out to be quite the mystery. I'd never been able to let go of a puzzle before I'd solved it, so my brain had been running nonstop since I took on the case.

I brushed my teeth, ran a brush through my hair, and slid on my favorite pair of tennis shoes.

I had a ton of things to do, starting with tracking down Melvin Harris. I needed to know if Lydia bought a cabin and, if so, check the place out. With any luck, I'd make it in and out of the cabin with less drama than when I'd investigated the Hatchett residence.

Mickey twined himself around my feet as I gave him some fresh food and water. I gave him a quick pat as he shoved his face into his bowl. I grabbed my purse and hurried out the door.

It was a long shot, but if Lydia had in fact purchased a cabin from Melvin, then there was a chance, a small chance but still a chance, that he might possibly know how often Lydia had visited the cabin and what she might have used it for. As far as I was concerned, she wasn't using it as a vacation house.

I got into my car and pulled out onto the street.

I didn't bother going in to the office. I wanted to get as much out of the day as possible, so I called to check in instead.

Mandy answered on the third ring.

"It's Barb. How's everything?"

"All is quiet here. How'd questioning the night manager go?" Mandy asked in her usual cheerful voice.

"She was sketchy to say the least," I answered. "But she did give me a lead. Tell me what you make of this," I said and then repeated what I'd learned from Melba as I turned off onto

Main Street and pointed my car in the direction of the nearest donut shop.

"Why would she need more than one room?" Mandy asked. "It's easy to assume that if she was meeting someone at the motel, then the manager didn't have to see the person she was meeting. He could've been waiting in the car or something. But more than one room? I don't get it. That situation doesn't sound like an affair to me."

"It doesn't sound like that to me, either," I admitted. "The manager, Melba, told me that the last time she saw Lydia, she was talking to a local contractor who's known to sell lakeside cabins. She said Lydia told her that it was time to move on."

"Why would she need a cabin out in the Grove?" Mandy asked.

"I don't know, but I need a favor."

"Sure. What do you need?" Mandy asked. I heard the shuffle of papers in the background. Mandy was one hell of a multitasker, and I admired her for it.

"I need to know of any property that Lydia might have purchased in the last two months. Especially anything out in Trinity Grove or the surrounding areas."

"I'm on it, boss," she said, and I heard the clickety-clack of the keyboard as Mandy went to work.

I stopped at the red light and tapped the fingertips of one hand against the steering wheel. Once the light changed to green I pulled into the drive-thru of the Happy Day Donut and Coffee Shop and ordered a bear claw and iced coffee while Mandy clacked away on the keyboard in search of answers.

I put the call on speakerphone and sat the cell phone in my empty cup holder, paid for my order, and pulled over into the parking lot where I parked my car in one of the only empty spots left.

I'd just bitten into my bear claw and swallowed when Mandy's voice came over the line.

"Lydia purchased a cabin in Trinity Grove two months ago."

"Well, that fits the timeline." I wiped my mouth on a pink napkin. "The motel receipts stop around that time, and that's when the night manager said she'd seen Lydia last. What else did you find?"

"Public records say that the cabin was built by Harris Construction. Melvin Harris is listed as the business owner. From what I can find, it looks like he's an upstanding business man," Mandy informed me. I heard more clicking in the background.

"His construction business is based out of Trinity Grove, and from the looks of it, is quite successful. He builds mostly summer homes and cabins around the area and some in the neighboring summer towns. He's married, has two teenage sons, and the most trouble he's ever been in is a few parking tickets when he was younger. Other than that, Melvin seems to be an ordinary guy and not much of a threat. I'll text you the cabin's address."

I wasn't about to ask how Mandy had gotten all of that information. Some things were better left unsaid.

"Great. Thanks, Mandy. You're a lifesaver."

"Hey, Barb," Kelly called out.

"Am I on speakerphone?" I asked.

"Yeah, Kelly just walked in and wanted to hear what was going on today."

"I'm heading back out to Trinity Grove right now to check out Lydia's cabin," I said.

"Why would Lydia want to buy a cabin out in the middle of nowhere when she and Robert have more vacation homes than they could ever use?" Kelly asked.

"I don't know. That's what has me stumped. I think that whatever she was doing or had going on inside those motel rooms and the reason she was interested in that cabin are the keys to why she was killed and who pulled the trigger."

"If you're headed back out to the Grove, why didn't you ask me to come along? I know you can take care of yourself, but we worry," Kelly said.

"I appreciate that, really, I do, but I need you two to stay at the office and do some work there. Call in some of the other clients whose cases we've wrapped up and give them the news. I'll be in as soon as I can."

"All right." Kelly sighed playfully. "But be sure you check in. I'm not going to relax unless I know you're safe."

"Will do, Mom," I joked. "I'll call you later."

I disconnected the call, slid the phone back into my purse, and finished off my bear claw. If two weeks ago you'd asked me what I saw myself doing today, I never would have said tracking down a killer to save my ex-fiancé's butt.

But, it is what it is.

I sat my coffee in the cup holder, backed out of the parking spot, and then pulled out onto the highway. I had another thirty-minute drive back out to the Grove. Even if I couldn't talk to Melvin today, I still had the address to the cabin, and I fully intended to see what that place was all about.

The drive to the Grove was surprisingly uneventful.

The speed limit lowered considerably as I rolled into the small town of Trinity Grove. I was amazed at how different it looked in the bright light of day. Family cars and SUV's were parked randomly in the parking lots of the mom-and-pop grocery store, drugstore, and even along the sides of the road. Some of the cars had kids and dogs hanging out of the windows like you'd see in an old summer movie, while others were topped with canoes and kayaks or pulled boats and Jet Skis behind them.

The town looked like a scene from a postcard straight out of the fifties. It was actually nice, peaceful even, with all the smiling faces and laughter everywhere I looked. I wondered for a second what it was like growing up in such a Hallmark-greeting-card type of scene as I drove through the town. Not that I hadn't enjoyed growing up with my mom. We'd lived in the city for as far back as I could remember, and even though I'd never known my dad, I didn't long for him to come find me.

My mom, my Aunt Hannah, and Aunt Mona were always there for me. Their influence was the reason I grew to be the person I was. They were my rocks.

Mona still was.

I pushed aside my moment of reminiscing, pulled up next to a small park, and then turned down my radio. I fished out the paper I'd scribbled Melvin's number on and dialed.

On the fifth ring I was beginning to wonder if anyone was going to pick up but then a friendly male voice answered. "Harris Construction, this is Melvin."

"Melvin, my name is Tina," I lied. "I was told that you had a secluded cabin you might be interested in selling."

"Well, I only had one cabin that I'd consider secluded here in Trinity Grove. If that's the one you're talking about, I'm sorry, but that property sold already. About two months ago, actually."

"Oh, that's too bad." I faked disappointment. "I understand that it was quite secluded, and that's exactly what I'm looking for. Something quiet and away from the city."

"I'm sorry, ma'am. If you're interested, I have other cabins around the Grove, but none are both secluded and lakefront as is the one you're interested in. I also build cabins if that's something that you'd be interested in?"

"It might be," I said. "Is there any way we can meet and discuss your properties?"

I knew the cabin had sold, but I needed a topic that would get him talking about that specific cabin and Lydia. Maybe he knew something about what she was doing out there.

"Sure," he said happily. "With the exceptions of a couple of meetings late this afternoon, I'm free until then. If you're close by I can meet you at Larry's Sandwich Shop for a late lunch. Is ten minutes good for you?"

"Sure. That sounds great. I'll meet you there."

We hung up, and I tossed my phone in my purse in the passenger seat. I pulled away from the park and back out onto the main street. Trinity Grove was about the size of a postage stamp, so instead of stopping and asking for directions, I just drove through town. The sandwich shop wasn't too difficult to find. I'd driven all of three minutes before I'd located Larry's.

The cute, little redbrick shop sat on the corner of Main Street and Broadway across from Manny's Sporting Goods.

While I waited for Melvin to arrive, I decided to call the office to check in.

Kelly answered on the second ring.

"How's it going?"

"Melvin agreed to meet me in about ten minutes. After I talk to him, I'm going to try to find the cabin. Mandy texted me the address, but I'm using Google Maps on my phone, and I don't know exactly where I'll have service out here. If I lose signal I'll just have to wing it."

I was the absolute worst at following directions. I could barely find my way home at the end of the day.

"I think that the motel and that cabin are linked to Lydia's death," Kelly said.

"That's what I think too," I agreed. "And that's exactly why I need to get inside that cabin."

"Before you hang up, there's something you need to know," Kelly said in a rush of words.

"What?" I asked. Kelly sounded a bit worried, so I knew that whatever she had to tell me couldn't be good. She wasn't the easily spooked type.

"Well," she began hesitantly. "Detective Black came in looking for you right after the first time you called this morning."

"What did he want?" I sat up straight in my seat and scanned the street, fully expecting to see the detective come rolling up beside me. A shiver of anticipation slid across my skin. I shook my head. Thinking about Black as anything more than a friendly pain in the rear at this point was absolutely ridiculous but apparently, if my dreams had anything to say about it, completely unavoidable.

I guess I'd just have to learn to go with it until I got him out of my system.

"He asked if you'd been in this morning. Apparently he went by your place, but you were already gone. I think you barely missed him on your way out to the Grove."

"Did you tell him where I was going?" I asked.

"Of course not. Who do you think you're talking to here?" She sounded affronted. "I told him that you called and said you had some things to take care of and that I didn't know how long it would take you or when you'd be back. I know he didn't believe me because he gave me that look. You know the one?" Kelly said.

"Oh, I know the look," I answered and drummed my fingers on the steering wheel. I'd seen that look a couple of times over our last meetings. So far, I'd discovered that Detective Black had two very effective looks. One could melt the panties off of a nun. The second...let's just say that you didn't want to be pinned with the second unless it was followed up by the first.

"I'll finish up with what I need to do here and hopefully make it back to the office before he discovers where I am. He's a great detective, so that probably won't take long. I shouldn't be more than a couple of hours. I have to go. I'll call you once I'm at the cabin."

I hung up and got out of the car. My loose teal top was starting to stick to my back with the rising afternoon heat. I reached behind me and pulled it away, then discreetly checked to make sure my gun was still tucked securely against the small of my back beneath the top where I always kept it hidden.

I stepped onto the sidewalk, around a group of board-shorts-wearing teens, and opened the door to the sandwich shop.

Larry's Sandwich Shop was quaint and much busier than I'd expected. The décor was done in a fifties diner theme with checkerboard tile, a long, black-topped bar, and red-and-chrome barstools. Surf memorabilia covered the walls. A pinball machine stood in the corner, and an old-time Coke bottle machine sat directly across from it. Several teens stood huddled around it like it was a totem to worship. I kind of expected to see those old singers Frankie and Annette step out of the back and start singing at any minute.

I squeezed into the only open corner booth next to the front window with a clear view of Main Street. I'd only been seated long enough to sit my purse down beside me in the seat when a large man made his way over to my table. He was tall, with a muscular build, short salt-and-pepper hair, a well-kempt beard and mustache, and sparkling green eyes. He was a handsome man to say the least.

His wife was a lucky woman.

"I'm Melvin Harris. You must be Tina?"

I nodded, remembering the false name I'd given him. "I am. How'd you know?"

He grinned and slid into the booth across from me. "I've lived in the Grove all of my life. I know just about everyone here, including most of the outsiders who frequent the town in the summers. Not to mention, I know everyone in this shop right now except for you." He grinned.

Melvin was charming. His grin was contagious, and I couldn't help but smile back at him.

"I see." I chuckled.

The waitress, a twenty-something redhead with legs to die for, came over and took our orders—two turkey club sandwiches with chips and Coke—then she hustled away.

"So, I understand that you're interested in a secluded cabin. Is that right?" Melvin cleared his throat and leaned back against the bench seat.

"It is." I nodded. "Melba down at the motel told me you had one available."

He tapped his fingers on the tabletop and laughed. "Melba. That woman's a piece of work."

"How so?" I asked.

"Telephone. Telegraph. Tele-Melba."

This time I laughed. "Oh, I see. Melba's who you need to go to if you want to get some information around here."

"Something like that." He nodded.

The waitress hurried over and sat our orders on the table in front of us, then rushed away.

Melvin took a drink of his Coke then peered at me.

"I have to wonder something though."

"What's that?" I asked.

"Melba knew that the particular cabin you're interested in already sold. Why would she tell you that it was still available?"

Good question. Melvin was a sharp cookie. I'd have to be careful with what I said to him. He was no pushover.

"I'm not sure." I sighed and pushed my food away. "I asked her if she knew of any secluded cabins available in the area. Something lakefront, away from any commotion. She told me the only one she knew of that fit my needs was one that you owned. She did say someone was interested in it a few months back, but she said that she didn't know if it sold or not." I rearranged my actual conversation with Melba and hoped he bought it. He must have because his expression softened, and he nodded as he ran a thumb over his beard.

"Well, Melba isn't known to be the most accurate source of information," he relented with a grin that lit up his whole face. "Oh, she'll hand it out, but that never means it's accurate. You just have to figure that part out for yourself."

Great. Everything Melba told me could've been complete nonsense.

"You said that the cabin sold," I began. "Is there any chance that the person who purchased it would be interested in selling?"

Melvin's face darkened. "I'm afraid I wouldn't know."

"Maybe I can talk to them and find out if they'd be interested in selling it? Could you possibly tell me who purchased it, and I can speak with them?"

I already knew who the buyer was, but I couldn't let Melvin know. If I did, then he'd start asking questions about me and my interest in Lydia, and that could potentially stop the flow of any information he could possibly give me.

He shook his head and set down his sandwich. "I'm afraid I can't tell you who purchased the place. I keep my clients' information private."

I started to ask another question, but he cut me off. "Even if I could tell you who bought the property, the information wouldn't help you. The person passed away not too long ago."

"Oh, I see." I faked surprise. "I'm so sorry to hear that. It's too bad they didn't get to enjoy their new summer home," I said then took a sip of soda.

"I wouldn't say they didn't get to enjoy it." He shook his head and took a bite of his sandwich.

"Why would you say that?" I asked curiously.

He swallowed his bite of food. "There're people there all the time. I see folks coming and going from the place when I drive past from other jobs out that way."

Who on Earth would be using Lydia's cabin, and would it hinder my scoping the place out?

"Oh, well, that's great." I smiled, but my mind was in a whirl.

Melvin finished the last bite of his sandwich and drink of soda.

"Listen, I have to get going. I have a meeting in about twenty minutes, but if you're still interested in buying or building I'd be more than happy to take a look at what I have available right now and get back to you if I have anything that fits your needs." He reached into the messenger bag he had sitting beside him, pulled out some pamphlets, and handed them to me.

I looked at the gorgeous cabins on the cover and nearly drooled.

"If you decide you'd like to build," he continued, "there are several different floor plans in there." He tapped a pamphlet on the tabletop. "And they're all fully customizable. We can install just about anything you could possibly want."

"These are gorgeous," I said in a state of awe. I was a city girl, but one of Melvin's cabins had the potential to change my mind.

"Thanks." He stood and smiled down at me. "I hate to hurry off, but I have to get going. I have your number in my phone from your call earlier. I'll give you a call if I have anything available fitting your needs, or you can give me a call if you decide that you'd rather build."

"Sounds good. Thanks again for meeting with me."

He shook my hand, tossed some money down on the table, then turned and made his way out of the shop.

I sat there for a minute and finished my late lunch, then called Kelly and told her what I'd learned.

"But getting inside the cabin might prove to be more complicated than I originally thought." I said.

"Why is that?" Mandy asked.

"Melvin said that he's seen people coming and going from the place since Lydia bought it, even *after* her death."

"Who else would know about the cabin, and who'd be spending time out there?" Mandy asked.

"I don't know, but I'm going to find out. Now I just have to find the place."

"We might be able to help you with that," Mandy said. "While you were meeting with Melvin I dug into his rental properties again. The property Lydia purchased is gated with two gates leading into the property and a tall, metal fence surrounding the property. One gate leads into the driveway, and the other is a side gate that leads out to the lake. Believe it or not, the place looks easy to find."

"What's the address again?"

She rattled off the address and some rough directions, and I jotted them down on a napkin so that I could input them into Google Maps on my phone.

"Thanks. I'm hoping to be back before nightfall. If I'm not, close up shop. I'll call when I get back into town, and we can meet up at my place to discuss what I find."

"I'll bring the pizza," Kelly said with a laugh.

"Be careful," Mandy warned.

"I will. Talk to you soon."

I disconnected the call.

I tossed a tip onto the tabletop since Melvin had paid for our lunches (what a gentleman), slid out of the booth, and hurried out to my car.

I fastened my seatbelt then keyed the address into Google Maps on my cell phone. I followed the monotone voice as it gave me directions, and nearly twenty minutes later I found myself in the middle of nowhere with spotty cell phone service just as I'd feared.

When I'd turned off the main road I had passed several cottages and campsites. Smiling people waved as I drove by. I was still thrown off by how friendly everyone was. The farther I drove, the more desolate the road became. Cabins and campsites became more and more scarce, then nonexistent. I glanced at my phone and wasn't surprised to see that I'd lost service altogether. I followed what I could see of the last image of the map still displayed on the screen of my phone.

I was beginning to think that I'd taken a wrong turn somewhere when the dirt road abruptly came to an end and turned into a smooth, short paved one.

I followed the short section of pavement and within minutes pulled up outside the double gate of a wrought-iron fence. This fence was much taller than the one surrounding Hatchett's estate and made a perfect square enclosure around a large, two-story log cabin. The lawn was perfectly groomed, and summer flowers sprouted in the flower beds lining the driveway, along a stone walkway up to the porch then around the house.

There were three cars in the driveway. The curtains on the second floor were drawn, so I couldn't see if there was any movement upstairs, but the bottom windows were wide open, and I spotted a man walking about inside.

I eased my car closer to the gate to get a better look and spotted an intercom system sticking out of the side of a stone pillar.

I wanted to get into the house and do a little investigating, but the fence's height and the inhabitants weren't the only things stopping me.

Much like the fence at Robert Hatchett's home, the one that had stolen the seat of my pants, this one had spikes lining the top, but where Hatchett's home fence had a space that I'd been able to slide between, this one had a line of several smaller spikes between the taller ones. There was no way to get over the fence unless I sprouted wings, and I was certain that wasn't something that was going to happen anytime soon no matter how much fried chicken I ate.

The only way in was if I broke in after nightfall, or if I found a way to walk through the front door.

I sat at the intercom for a moment and tried to decide what I was going to do. I needed inside that place and the sooner the better but under what guise? I had an idea. It was thinner than Trump's comb-over, but I didn't really have any other choice. I gathered up my courage and pressed the intercom button.

"May I help you?"

I was startled by the deep rumble of a male voice.

"I'm Barb. I um—"

"Do you have an appointment?"

Appointment? To what? For what?

"I'm a friend of Lydia's." I said the first thing that popped into my mind. It was all I had in my arsenal at the time.

"I'll open the gate."

I couldn't believe my ears, and a second later the gate slid open, allowing me entry.

I took a deep breath, drove through the gate, and parked behind a gleaming white Mercedes that happened to be parked beside a solid black Jaguar. Needless to say, my red Beetle stuck out like a sore thumb. It was ridiculous, but I felt like the other cars were laughing at me. Like they knew full well that I didn't belong here doing this. Whatever *this* actually was.

Getting in the gate was easier than I'd expected, but I didn't expect my luck to hold out. Getting into the house probably wouldn't be as easy. I grabbed my purse, stepped out of my car, bumped the door shut with my hip, and climbed the steps up to the porch. A cool, late-summer breeze blew through my hair as I approached the door. I'd just raised my hand to knock when the door opened, and I was met by what I could only describe as a shirtless Adonis.

Seriously. An *Adonis*.

The man standing in the doorway was absolutely amazing. He wore only loose-fitting, grey cotton pajama pants, and his feet were bare. His hair was a shimmering black, his eyes, blue, and my goodness, he had abs that would've made Hercules himself weep. I wanted to reach out and poke one of them just to see if it felt as hard as it looked.

I was taken aback by the brilliantly white, welcoming smile that he tossed my direction as I stood gaping at him like a crazy person. I was there to get to the bottom of a murder, but what I really wanted to do was throw myself into his arms and let him cart me into that big cabin to do with as he saw fit.

Too long without a man was making me crazy.

Calm down, woman, I chided myself with an inner shake and tried to gather my wits.

"You're a friend of Lydia's?" Mr. Sexy asked.

I nodded, still not quite able to trust any words to come out of my mouth.

"Well please, come in." He stood to the side and waved me past with a large, well-manicured hand. His hands were beautiful.

I stepped past him into the entry.

The interior of the cabin was absolutely gorgeous. Dark wood ran throughout the open floor plan. Dark red curtains hung over the windows, and neutral-colored, overstuffed furniture littered the living space.

"This place is beautiful," I said once I was able to trust myself to speak without making a complete fool out of myself.

"Thanks. I'm Silas, and you said your name was?" he asked while making his way into the kitchen to the refrigerator.

"Barb," I cleared my throat.

"Have a seat, Barb." He grinned at me over his muscular shoulder and pointed to a long breakfast bar.

I walked over to the stool and set my purse on the countertop beside me, then slid onto a stool.

Silas reached into the refrigerator and pulled out a bottle of water, then set it before me on the glistening black granite countertop.

He leaned his backside against the opposite countertop and eyed me suspiciously.

"You said you're a friend of Lydia's. How did you know her exactly?"

I took a drink of the bottled water he'd given me and got myself back into investigator mode.

"She and I met at one of her charity functions about a month ago," I lied.

"I see." He rubbed one long finger across his full bottom lip. "And she told you about this place?" he asked. The smile never left his face. "About us?"

I had no idea what he was talking about, but I nodded anyway.

"Uh-huh, she did."

"Is everything all right down there, Si?"

I turned at the sound of another man's voice, and much to my surprise found another work of art staring down at us over the balcony railing. This man had a darker complexion, short-cropped hair, and sported the same drool-worthy body as my host, Silas.

I had to stop myself from sighing aloud.

"Everything's fine, Max. I was just having a talk with my new friend Barb, here." He motioned to me, and his grin deepened.

What on Earth was going on here? I tried to take in my surroundings, but nothing other than the incredibly hot men seemed odd.

The man I now knew as Max eyed me warily, then turned and reentered what I assumed was one of the bedrooms.

Maybe these guys were a couple?

"It's sad what happened to Lydia." Silas's voice drew my attention back to him. "It was a shame." He continued. "She was such a wonderful woman." His gaze held me in place.

"I can't imagine who would've wanted to kill her."

I watched him closely.

"No. Neither can I. You must've known Lydia pretty well for her to tell you about this place."

"We were becoming close just before she passed."

If he knew Lydia as well as he appeared to, then he knew that the chances of Lydia and I being friends were slim to none. I needed to get as much information from Silas as I could before he discovered why I was really sitting on his barstool and threw me out on my rear.

Silas continued to study me from beneath long, thick, black lashes that I'd give up a couple of toes to possess.

"She didn't have any enemies that I know of, but like I said, I was just getting to know her. Do you think it was personal?"

"I wouldn't know." He shrugged his lightly tanned shoulders.

He prowled around the bar and took a step toward me, then another and another, until he stood so close to me that I could smell his heady cologne and feel the heat of his bare chest against my covered one.

"Let's cut the chatter." He brushed the hair away from my face. "Lydia handled all of the scheduling and monetary transactions, but since she passed, we've been a little out of sorts. I thought my day was clear today, but then you showed up on our doorstep, so you must've had an appointment I missed. Lydia wouldn't have told you about this place unless she trusted you."

I stared up at this big hunk of man twirling my hair around his finger with what I was certain was a dumfounded expression. What the heck was he talking about? Scheduling? Monetary transactions?

"You obviously like what you see." He grinned down at me. "And I'm pretty impressed with you myself." He gave me a slow once over. "Not all women who come here for our attentions are tens, but you..." He trailed the pad of his thumb over my jawline. "I'm definitely going to enjoy you, and I guarantee you're in for the time of your life."

What in the hell was happening? I blinked up at him, completely lost as to what the heck he was talking about. What had I gotten myself into?

The thought had just stomped through my mind when he grasped the back of my neck in his big, hot palm, and before I could protest (not that I'm sure I actually would have), his lips landed on mine in a searing hot kiss that I felt all the way down to the tips of my toes.

His tongue slipped in and slid against mine, and I was on the verge of being hopelessly lost. It took a moment for my brain to reengage, but once it did, I knew that if I didn't stop Silas and find out what exactly was going on here, I was going to be in some serious trouble. Pleasurable trouble but trouble nonetheless.

I pressed a hand against his chest and leaned back away from his fiery kiss. He peered down at me with confusion but didn't resist. He looked like he was surprised that I'd actually told him no, but before he could question my seemingly odd behavior, a door closed overhead, and giggling drifted down to us.

I looked up and saw a tall woman with auburn hair come practically skipping down the stairs. Max followed along behind her. She carried her high heels in one hand, her purse in the other, and her clothing was just the slightest bit rumpled.

It was the walk of shame.

I'd seen it a million times in college. This mystery woman and Max had just gotten lucky.

"Same time next week?" he asked. She giggled and nodded. Max smiled, opened the door for her, and saw her out to her car.

Same time next week?

A sexually satisfied woman?

Scheduling.

Monetary transactions.

A large residence secluded away from prying eyes.

What Silas meant when he mentioned women coming to him for services.

Suddenly it all became clear.

I was in a brothel. I was in a male brothel full of gigolos!

I stared up at the rooms and watched as two more outrageously attractive men led one woman to a room from the back of the house, and then another man led another woman down the stairs and out onto the patio.

Holy Nikes. Lydia was running a male brothel. That's what she'd been doing in the motel and why she wanted the cabin to be secluded. Women from the city could come out to the Grove and see their stud without running the risk of someone seeing them. And with Lydia supposedly being a homebody, no one would ever guess that she was at the helm.

The entire idea was actually a stroke of genius. I had to give Lydia props.

"Is something wrong?" Silas asked as I hopped off of the stool like something had just shot me in the bum.

"No, nothing. I just... I need to go. I'm sorry."

"Are you all right?" he asked, his voice full of concern.

I looked up at him then at the entryway where Max had returned and was watching us intently.

"I'm fine. I just—I have to go. I'm sorry." I wiggled my way out of the hot, firm grip he had on my waist and made a beeline for the door.

I fished my keys out of my pocket, hopped into my car, passed through the gate, and sped back toward the office. I couldn't wait to tell the girls what I'd found at the cabin. Lydia had been a naughty girl.

* * *

I'd left the cabin so quickly, excited to have found out what Lydia was into, that I'd gotten turned around on my way back to the main road. Night was starting to fall as I finally found my way back onto the main street of Trinity Grove. I followed the road leading out of town and turned on my headlights. It was then that I realized that I'd left my purse behind at the cabin. What had I been thinking? How could I have been so careless?

Normally, I always left it in the car. I had no idea what had possessed me to take it inside with me. I'd been kicking myself since I'd glanced over and realized it wasn't in the seat beside me. Thank goodness I had slid my phone and car key in my jeans pocket.

I couldn't believe what I'd just discovered.

Lydia was a madam. She ran what I'd just dubbed a stud farm. Brothel just sounded so snooty.

How had she kept something like that a secret? My recent discovery answered a few of my question and added what felt like a million more. How many more layers of Lydia Hatchett were there to discover?

Charities, affairs, a stud farm.

She'd been a busy woman. How had she even had time to comb her hair, much less still be able to keep up the pretense that she was a homebody-housewife, I wondered.

Darkness crept over the landscape as the last rays of daylight faded. I couldn't wait to get back to my place, call the girls, and share what I'd just discovered.

I pulled to the side of the road and fired off a text to both Mandy and Kelly telling them to meet me at the office first thing in the morning because I had big news to share.

I slid my phone back into my pocket and pulled back out onto the road.

Mandy and Kelly would never believe it. I cranked up the radio and settled in for the long drive back to the city.

I was about fifteen minutes outside the Grove, speeding down the road with a million questions rolling through my head and a Lenny Kravitz song blasting through the speakers, when a pair of headlights illuminated my car from behind.

The bright beams lit up the interior of my Beetle like a spotlight. I tried to ignore the blinding light, but it was impossible. I figured the speeding vehicle behind me was just some teens out for a joyride or something of that nature. It was the end of summer after all.

I kept my eye on the road and hoped the truck would pass me soon. That hope was short-lived. The truck accelerated and, before I had time to react, slammed into my back bumper.

I couldn't have been more wrong. Whoever was driving that truck was no fun-seeking teenager.

My tiny car took a sharp swerve to the right. I held the steering wheel in a death grip and fought to keep my Beetle on the road and out of the deep culvert alongside it. The truck ramming into me was large and black or dark blue in color. I couldn't be certain.

The headlights were too bright for me to see who was driving, but at the moment, I didn't care. All I wanted was to get out of the situation alive.

The engine of the truck roared as it picked up speed to ram into me again. I ground my teeth together and braced for impact. The truck accelerated and slammed into me harder this time. My tiny car flung forward, tires screeching as I struggled to stay on the blacktop. Even though I had the accelerator pressed all the way to the floor, I was now moving at a much slower pace than before. I heard the sound of metal grinding against rubber. I chanced a look in the side mirror and realized why.

My rear fenders were smashed and crumpled in against the tires, causing my speed to decrease. The smell of burning rubber reached my nose. I could hear my bumper scraping against the asphalt and knew it was hanging by a thread.

But that was the least of my problems.

My steering wheel would only turn to the right. I fought with all of my strength to keep the car in my lane and out of the culvert. My muscles screamed in protest as I pulled the wheel to the left in an effort to keep the car headed straight on the highway. My gaze zeroed in on the bridge up ahead.

I was in one hell of a predicament. My car was totaled, the truck was three times the size of my little bug, and the driver, whoever he was, obviously wanted me dead. I glanced out the passenger side window at the deep culvert to my right, then ahead at the upcoming bridge. If I let the wheel go, the car would veer off to the right. My arm strength was zapped, and the car was starting to veer to the right despite my best efforts to keep it from doing so.

Either I could let go of the wheel and take my chances hitting the deep culvert, or I could keep going and ultimately hit the bridge.

I'd heard people talk about their life flashing before their eyes when in a life-or-death situation, and I'd always called it bullcorn...until now.

In a flash, I saw myself laughing with Kelly and Mandy over wine and pizza in front of the television. I saw the smile on my face the day my office opened. I saw my cat Mickey nuzzling me with his little nose, and out of nowhere, I saw Detective Black's mischievous grin just before he kissed me.

I had a sinking feeling that I'd always regret not having the chance to experience that last item...or maybe not.

I didn't want to die, and I'd be darned if I let some schmuck take my life before I was finished living it.

I took a deep breath. I would not die tonight.

The driver of the truck saw his opportunity to slam into me again and took it.

Only this time I saw him coming.

I had two choices. Turn the wheel to the right and aim for the culvert when he hit me or slam head-on into the bridge. The way I saw it, there was only one option that I could possibly live through. I took a deep breath and braced myself for impact.

The truck smashed into my car one final time. My head slammed into the side window, but I let go of the wheel, and it spun hard to the right. My tiny Beetle hit the side of the road and was airborne, then flipped in midair before landing in the ditch on its top.

I was surprised that the roof hadn't caved in on impact and that I was still alive. I was hanging upside down from my seatbelt. I was still conscious but just barely. I'd never again roll my eyes when a car salesman prattled on about the five-star crash rating.

My vision was blurry. I fished around on the roof of the car where all of my belongings now rested and nearly wept with joy when my hand connected with my cell phone. I heard the truck slowly approaching. I had no idea who was behind the wheel of that vehicle, but I knew without a doubt that his intentions were to kill me.

The vehicle stopped. I heard it idling and listened for the door to open.

My mind went into a tailspin. I felt around on the roof of the car but couldn't find my gun. I'd taken it out of the waist of my pants and set it in the passenger seat while I drove.

What if whoever was behind the wheel of that truck got out and made sure he finished the job? Did he have a gun? A knife?

I opened my one unswollen eye and dialed 9-1-1. Before the dispatcher answered, I heard the truck roar by. He hadn't gotten out. I guess he figured he'd accomplished what he'd set out to do.

"9-1-1. What is your emergency?"

"I've been in an accident..."

CHAPTER SIX

———

His nametag read Dr. Richard Hope, but it should've read Dr. Hotty McHotterson.

I was starting to sweat just being in the same vicinity as the incredibly hot emergency room doctor while he finished wrapping my right wrist in an ACE bandage.

"Just a few seconds and you'll be all done."

I hadn't been to a lot of emergency rooms in my life, but I was fairly certain not all doctors looked like the hunk of hotness seated on a low stool before me. I expected to see a short, round man with grey hair wearing a long white coat. Instead I got mister tall-tan-and-handsome in a pair of well filled-out, dark blue scrubs.

To say that I was pleasantly surprised would be an understatement.

"I don't think I've ever treated a female private investigator before. This is a first for me."

"I'm so happy to be the one to pop your female private eye cherry," I joked.

He laughed a deep, rumbling laugh that warmed my insides.

"Sassy," he teased with a saucy wink of his own.

It had been a long time since I'd indulged in a little harmless flirtation, especially with someone as hunktastic as the doc. I forgot how good it felt.

"The good thing is that your wrist isn't broken, but it *is* severely sprained and will be sore for a couple of weeks." He secured the bandage. "You're lucky. You could have been killed." He reached up and smoothed my hair off the giant bruise making itself at home along one side of my forehead.

"That's a nasty bruise, but the scan didn't show anything serious." He checked the chart. "You'll have a headache for a couple of days. Ibuprofen should help with any pain, but if you experience any dizziness, nausea, or vomiting, you need to get back here immediately."

"Thanks." I attempted a smile. "Honestly, being run off the road isn't a common occurrence. As a matter of fact, this is the first time anything like this has ever happened to me."

He shook his head, and I took a second to appreciate his sharp profile. The doctor had the most mesmerizing blue eyes and full lips. His pale blond hair was slightly shaggy, as though he was a couple of weeks late for a trim. He was hands-down one of the handsomest men I'd ever seen.

"But that's exactly what happened, isn't it?" he asked seriously. "Hopefully it won't happen again." His eyes met mine. "I'd like to keep you here overnight for observation, but you made your dislike of hospitals abundantly clear when the ambulance brought you in." I saw him struggling not to smile at the memory. "So, since your scan didn't show any fractures or internal bleeding, I'm not going to force the issue." He gave up and grinned.

I hated the thought of staying in the hospital more than I hated the *Jersey Shore* reality show I'd had the displeasure of stumbling upon late one night. I hadn't watched television for a month after coming across that little piece of WTF.

"Thank you. I really would rather nurse my wounds in the comfort of my own home."

He nodded his blond head. "That's what I thought you'd say."

"A cup of hot chocolate and a snuggle with my cat, and I'll be as good as new."

"A snuggle, huh?" Dr. Hope smiled up at me, and my skin tingled. Not only was the good doctor handsome, he was charming.

The curtain separating us from the rest of the emergency room was ripped back. The metal curtain hooks screeched their protest against the rail, and I had to fight the urge to grit my teeth and cover my ears.

"What in the hell happened?"

I jumped as Detective Black barged past the curtain.

The doc stood up between us and raised his palms in an attempt to stop the detective's advance. "I'm sorry, but you can't be in here."

"The hell I can't." Black held up his badge, and the doctor dropped his hands to his sides.

"I need to ask Ms. Jackson some questions, starting with *what in the hell* she was doing alone on that lone stretch of highway so late at night."

I scowled. Who in the heck did he think he was? Barging into the hospital, interrupting the only flirting session with a sexy man (not counting Silas. That situation was a bit one-sided.) I'd had in what felt like ages, and grilling me like I was a common criminal in front of said sexy man? The last time I checked, I was the victim in all of this.

"She needs to rest, and I don't care who you are. You're not just going to barge in here and yell at my patient." Dr. Hope stood his ground. "She's been through a lot tonight—"

"I was doing my job." I cut the doctor off. "And the last time I checked, it was perfectly acceptable for a woman to drive alone at night. This isn't the early nineteen fifties, in case you haven't noticed, and I don't need a babysitter."

"Yes, I'm fully aware that you're grown and what year it happens to be." Detective Black glared at me around the doctor. "That's not what I'm talking about. I'm talking about the fact that you didn't bother to tell anyone where you were going."

"I'm sorry, but I don't have to report in to anyone, especially you." I pointed at him with my uninjured hand. "And for your information, *Detective*, Mandy knew exactly where I was going."

He growled. Actually growled. Like a caveman.

It was hot and irritating and confusing all at the same time.

"But you still chose to go *alone*?"

"Seriously, Detective—"

"Tyler." He interrupted me.

"What?" I frowned at his interruption.

"My name is Tyler." He ran a hand through his hair with frustration. "Call me crazy, but I have a feeling that I'll be dealing with you and your irresponsible antics a lot more in the future, so we might as well get on a first-name basis with each other."

I shook off the snide remark and continued my rant. I was on a roll, and there was no stopping me once I got started. I was almost killed, had a serious headache, my car was totaled, and I was late to feed Mickey which meant that he was probably taking a poo in my favorite shoes as we spoke.

"*Tyler.*" I practically groaned. "I'm a grown woman. I think I can take care of myself."

"Like you did tonight?" he snapped. "I told you to be careful, to watch your back, but did you listen? *Nooo.*" He tossed his hands into the air. "You just went off and did as you saw fit. Do you ever stop to think about your own safety?"

The doctor stood looking back and forth between us like he was watching a ping-pong ball.

This time I growled, but Tyler ignored me. He was the one on a roll now, and I was just about fed up with his high-handed behavior. He was ranting so hard that he was starting to resemble an irate teenage girl who'd lost her favorite T-shirt, and I was getting seriously annoyed.

I briefly wondered what kind of jail time I would be looking at if I kneed him in that big set of balls he obviously had.

"All right, that's enough."

As soon as the words were out of the doctor's mouth I wondered if he had a death wish. The look Tyler bestowed upon him was so anger-filled it would've scared Manson himself, but the doc ignored it.

"Ms. Jackson was—"

"Barb. Call me Barb."

The doc cast a quick glance in my direction then looked back at Tyler. "Barb was just in an accident. She's injured, shaken, and the last thing she needs is for you or anyone else to come in here bullying her. I don't care if you're a cop, her parents, or the pope himself. You will not harass her. She needs rest and someone to care for her instead of nagging her about what she should've done and what could've happened."

Tyler stepped forward and visibly clenched his jaw.

"I'm not bullying her." He took a deep breath. "Someone tried to kill her because of a case she's working. *My* case, to be exact. Now, because of her recklessness"—he jabbed a finger at me—"it's *my* job to keep her safe."

"Excuse me, but I was not being reckless." I tried to interject, but it was like I wasn't even in the room. The men were too busy comparing the sizes of each other's package to even notice me anymore.

Tyler's dark complexion and thick muscular frame facing off against Dr. Hope's light, leaner muscular frame was quite a sight to behold.

I have to admit, being witness to the two hottest men I'd seen in a long time face-off was a bit of a turn on. Now all I needed was Silas to show up shirtless with his sexy grin, and I could sell tickets.

I seriously needed to get out more.

"Good. See that you do," the doc said then turned to me. "Do you feel safe alone with this man?"

I peered up into the doctor's concerned blue eyes then chanced a peek at the detective. While Tyler looked more than a bit ticked off, I couldn't gather a sliver of fear of him.

I nodded. "He's not as bad as he seems." I winked at the doc. He smiled, then fished in the pocket of his scrubs and pulled out a card. He scribbled something on the back then handed the little slip to me.

"That's my cell number on the back. If you need anything, don't hesitate to call."

I took the card and smiled as he tossed a wink at me, glowered at Tyler, and then turned to leave.

He grasped the curtain, then turned back to me.

"I meant it when I said if you need *anything*. Just give me a call. You can sign your discharge papers at the desk on your way out."

Tyler growled. I blushed, and the doc grinned.

Once the doctor was out of the room, Tyler pulled the curtain shut and took a seat next to me on the bed.

He ran his hand through his hair and took a deep calming breath. When he spoke again, his tone was much softer.

"I just saw your car, Barb. You have no idea how lucky you are to be alive."

"I have an idea," I said.

He reached up and swiped his thumb over the bruise on my forehead, then jerked his hand back as though he caught himself doing something wrong, but his expression softened. "Are you really all right?"

"I was a lot better before you came in here yelling at me and stomping around like a bull."

Tyler frowned at me. "I didn't mean to yell at you, but you have to understand. You could've been killed. I think whoever ran you off the road had that express intent in mind."

I knew that what he said was true, but someone trying to kill me just didn't make a lick of sense. Who was driving that truck, and why were they out to kill me? Perhaps I'd gotten too close to the truth about Lydia's murder without knowing it. That theory was a long shot as I'd just started working the case and thus far had diddly-squat to go on other than Lydia was apparently a madam, but it was still an option worth considering.

Mainly because it was the only option I had.

I sat that curiosity on the back burner for later examination and nodded at Tyler.

"When I saw your car, I thought there was no way you could've survived. You scared me to death," he murmured and looked away from me.

"You barely know me."

He smiled and chuckled. "I know, but what can I say?" He shrugged. "You're a hard woman to forget, Barb. I hate to admit it, but I haven't been able to get you out of my mind since I saw you in the police station."

I felt a blush rise in my cheeks and glanced away. What was I supposed to say to that? A man I barely knew, a man I was more attracted to than any man I'd ever known, had just confessed that he couldn't stop thinking about me. Was worried about me.

I didn't know what to say or do, so I just sat there like a lump. Wasn't it just like a man to add more fuel to the fire of my already-addled brain?

Tyler rubbed his hands together like he didn't know what to do with them, then stood up in front of me and shoved them into his pockets.

"I know what you mean," I said and looked away. There had barely been a minute since I'd met him that I'd been able to stop thinking about him.

"But you don't have to tell me how lucky I am. I was in that car, in case you've forgotten."

"Believe me, I haven't forgotten." He regarded me seriously. "I don't think I'll ever forget."

I didn't know what it was about this man I barely knew, but he had me twisted in knots. I couldn't decide if I wanted to throw myself into his arms or run as far away as possible.

For the moment, I'd settle for a steaming hot bath.

"I have some questions for you about what happened."

"Can we do this back at my place?" I asked. "I'd really rather get the heck out of here. These places give me the heebie-jeebies."

Tyler laughed. "I understand completely. Sure." He smiled down at me. "We can get out of here. I'll call and let the station know that I'm taking your statement in-home so that you can get some rest instead of sitting at the station all night."

"Thanks. I really do appreciate it."

Tyler held out his hand. I took it and hopped off the edge of the bed.

"You're welcome. Now seeing as how your car is completely demolished and we're both going to the same place, I take it that you're fine with me driving you home?"

"Honestly, I couldn't care less who drives me as long as I get there soon...and in one piece," I added as an afterthought. "There's a pair of yoga pants in the dryer, a leftover cheesecake in the fridge calling my name, and I might have a little time to feed Mickey before he makes a poo in my shoes."

"Come again?"

I shook my head. "Never mind. Let's get out of here."

He looked at me, shook his head, and chuckled. "All right. Let's get you home."

We turned to leave, but the curtain was jerked back for a second time. This time it was Kelly who barged in asking questions.

"Oh, my goulash! What in the heck happened? I would've been here sooner, but my cell phone service is janky in my new apartment. All I understood were the words Barb and hospital," she rambled.

I'd called Kelly while in the ambulance instead of Mona simply because I didn't want Mona to have a heart attack. I'd call her first thing in the morning

"I'm fine," I assured her as she pulled me in for a bear hug that made me wince. Apparently the fact that I had been in an accident hadn't sunk in just yet.

"I didn't even know which hospital you were in. My stupid phone was breaking up while you were talking. I just started here because it was closest and hoped for the best."

She held me at arm's length and gave me a once-over. "Are you hurt?"

"Just a little banged up, but I'll be fine after a good night's sleep," I assured her.

I took a look at Kelly. I wasn't sure she looked any better than I did. Her normally sleek black hair looked like a couple of birds had turned it into their love nest. Bags had started to form under her eyes, and she had not a stitch of makeup on.

Bottom line? Kelly looked like an extra from *Night of the Living Dead*, but I wasn't one to talk. I could only imagine how I looked after my little near-death experience.

Kelly blew out a relieved breath then gestured in Tyler's general direction. "What's Captain America doing here?"

I fought the urge to laugh at Tyler's less-than-thrilled expression at Kelly's description of him.

"He thinks that my accident tonight has something to do with our case."

"Really?" she gasped. "Well, did you tell him that he's wrong? This was just an accident." She looked from me to Tyler, then back to me. "Wasn't it?"

I bit my bottom lip and looked away.

As much as I wanted to tell Kelly that the accident and my investigating the case were just a coincidence, I couldn't. What were the chances, really?

"Barb? This was just an accident, wasn't it?" she asked again forcefully. Worry etched itself across her face as she awaited my answer.

"Not exactly," I finally admitted.

"And what *exactly* does that mean?"

"She was run off the road between here and Trinity Grove." Tyler chose that moment to speak up.

"What?" she nearly shrieked. "I should've gone with you. I knew that I shouldn't have let you go out there alone." She tossed her hands in the air.

"I thought Mandy was the mother of this group?" I joked. "And like I told Tyler, it's not the fifties."

"That's not what I mean, and you know it." Kelly propped her hand on her hip. "Now, Seriously, Barb. Answers, please."

I knew she was worried about me, so I ignored her tone.

"I didn't need you to go with me," I said calmly. "Besides, who knows what would have happened to you had you gone with me. You could've been seriously injured, and I couldn't live with that."

She reached out and hugged me again, then released me and stepped back.

"I'm just glad that you're okay." She sniffled.

I reached up and rubbed the bruised knot on my forehead with the tips of my fingers. I had one heck of a headache and more questions than answers. I knew these two had every right to question me. They cared about me, but I wanted nothing more than to go home and sleep for a few days.

"Listen, you two," I said quietly. "I'll answer all of your questions, but I really need to get out of here." I slid my uninjured hand into my front pocket then looked at Kelly. "Tyler was just about to drive me home. Would you like to meet us there? I'm pretty sure that the two of you have mostly the same questions, and I'd like to take a shot at only answering them once if at all possible."

Kelly and Tyler exchanged a look then Kelly nodded. "Let's go. My car is out front." She grabbed my arm.

"She's riding with me. That hasn't changed," Tyler said, and from the tone of his voice, there was no room for argument. After the day that I'd had, I couldn't care less who gave me a ride home as long as I got there in one piece.

"Well, all right then," Kelly said. "I'll meet you at your place in about ten minutes. I really should call Mandy and let her know what's happening. I'll also let her know that you won't be coming in tomorrow, so she and I will need to cancel your least important appointments and handle the rest ourselves."

"Thank you." I sighed with relief. "I just have to sign the discharge papers, and we'll meet you at my house. Drive safe."

The joke was on her. Unless hell froze over, there was no way I wasn't going in to the office in the morning. I had too much to tell them and a murder that I was one step closer to solving.

Kelly gave me one last quick hug, eyed Tyler with a hint of irritation, and then hurried down the hall toward the exit, dialing her phone as she went.

CHAPTER SEVEN

"What can you tell me about the car that ran you off of the road? On second thought"—Tyler held up his hand—"just go back to the beginning. Why were you out in Trinity Grove?"

The three of us had made it back to my place in record time. Tyler and I had made it back so quickly because Tyler drove like a madman, and that was putting it mildly. Richard Petty would've been proud.

I had to remind him several times that I'd already been in one accident this evening, and I didn't want to be in another. Of course he ignored me and continued to drive as he pleased.

Kelly, however, must've sprouted wings out of her backside and flew because she was on my front porch waiting when we pulled up in Tyler's black SUV by the curb. I would've nagged her about her reckless speeding, but it would've gone in one ear and out the other just as it had with Tyler. That's just how Kelly was.

I sat propped against one end of my overstuffed sofa with a fluffy blanket over my lap.

If I didn't have a nagging detective questioning me, and a hovering best friend staring at me like I was about to drop dead at any minute, life would be great.

I arranged my favorite fluffy blanket around my legs and took a sip of the salted caramel hot cocoa Kelly had handed me.

The hot cocoa part of her hovering I didn't mind.

"I was following a lead on my case, and it led me out to Trinity Grove."

Tyler cocked a brow at me. "You mean *my* murder case?"

"Your murder case. My murder case." I shrugged. "Let's not spilt hairs." I blew gently on my hot cocoa.

"Come on, Barb. Cut the bull," Tyler said wearily. "I know you have a strict confidentiality rule about your cases and clients, but it's not like I don't already know what you're up to. This is an open murder investigation. I need to know what you've found out so far in case it's pertinent to the investigation. I need to find Lydia Hatchett's killer and keep you from joining her on the list of victims."

I regarded him for a second over the rim of my mug then took a comforting sip. In all honesty, I hadn't found much of anything in the way of evidence leading to who could've killed Lydia Hatchett. I wanted to think that the stud farm had something to do with it all, but I didn't have a stitch of hard evidence.

As much as I wanted to tell him that I'd found a boatload of evidence, I just couldn't.

"All right, how about this?" He leaned his brawny forearms against his knees and tapped his pen against the pad of paper he held. "We'll share."

"Share?" Kelly and I said in unison.

"Yeah. We'll share evidence." He looked from her to me. "Here's what I suggest," he began. "I'll share as much about the case as I can without risking my job or jeopardizing the case, and you can share what you've found with me," he proposed.

Was he serious? I stared at him in open-mouthed shock for longer than I would've liked and longer than I was sure was attractive, but I was at a loss for words.

I leaned over and set my mug of cocoa on the table.

"Why the change of heart all of a sudden?"

He splayed his hands palms up in front of him. "Because I know you're not going to let this case go." His eyes met mine. "Especially not after what happened tonight. So what do you say? We share?"

I glanced at Kelly. She shrugged. "I say spill it, Barb. You were almost killed. Tonight was too close a call. What would it hurt to share information? At least he's willing to now, when before he wouldn't even let you see a simple file."

She was right. Tyler was a great detective. If he had evidence that I didn't, which I knew he did—like I said, he was a great detective—and he shared that evidence with me, it was possible that I could wrap up this case before Jason went to jail.

"All right. You first," I said.

My cat Mickey chose that moment to jump his big coal-black self onto my lap for some love. I scratched his head, and he curled into a ball on my lap, making himself at home.

Tyler leaned back into the chair and ran his fingers through his inky black hair. He looked a bit disheveled, but who was I to judge? It was after two in the morning, and who knew how long it had been since he'd been to bed. I certainly didn't look my best. I took a second longer to admire him. Even though he looked a little rough, he was still the handsomest man I'd ever seen.

"This morning I responded to a call that led me to an alley behind the Thai restaurant over on Fifth Street," he began. "Turns out one of the cooks who works there was taking out the trash and found a gun lying on the ground beside the dumpster. From the position of the gun it looked like someone was in a hurry and tried to toss it in, but missed."

"Like they were running and tossed it at the can without looking?" I asked.

Tyler nodded.

"What kind of gun was it?" Kelly asked.

"It was a nine-millimeter handgun, just like the one that killed Lydia Hatchett," he confirmed.

"Did you pull any prints? Did the bullet from Lydia match the gun?" I fired off questions.

He nodded. "Yes. Ballistics came back this evening just before I heard about your *accident*. Striations on the barrel match the ones found on the bullet that killed Lydia. It's without a doubt our murder weapon, but there weren't any prints, and the serial number was ground off, so there's no way to find out who the weapon belonged to."

"Jason isn't a registered gun owner, so that's good news for him," Kelly said and crossed her legs in the oversized chair as she sat up a little straighter. "But then again, he still could've purchased the gun illegally and killed Lydia."

I cast her a sarcastic *thanks-a-million-for-your-help* expression, and she grinned. I was trying to get Jason out of a murder charge, not dig the hole he was in deeper.

I continued petting Mickey's head. He opened one eye, looked up at me with an uninterested expression, closed it, and then rested his head back on my thigh. Some help he was.

"Now." Tyler reached over and tapped my toes with his pen to get my attention. "What were you doing out in Trinity Grove?" he asked, then moved from his chair and took a seat on the end of the sofa I was seated on. He reached over and gave Mickey a scratch behind the ears. Mickey opened his eyes, peered at Tyler for less than a minute with the same bored, uninterested expression he'd given me, then reclosed his eyes, and started purring.

Purring.

Mickey was more the scratchy-bleedy type when it came to his attitude with strangers.

Why was he purring? The little traitor. Even my cat wasn't immune to Tyler's charm.

I blew out a frustrated breath. "The day I paid a visit to Hatchett's home—"

"The day you broke in, you mean?" The corner of Tyler's mouth quirked up.

"Whatever." I brushed his interruption away, and he chuckled. "I found some receipts in a hidden cubby in the bottom of Lydia's nightstand."

"How'd you find the cubby?"

"The bottom sounded hollow when I knocked on it." I shrugged.

Tyler jotted down some notes. "Are you sure that the nightstand you were rifling through didn't belong to Robert?" he asked, then reached for his cup of cocoa and raised the cup to his lips.

"Let's just say that the contents of the opposite nightstand told me loud and clear who it belonged to. Unless I'm mistaken and Lydia Hatchett had some use for a bottle of *Jerkins* lotion and a Blu-ray copy of *Busty MILFS IV*"

Tyler nearly choked on his cocoa and quickly grabbed a napkin from the table. Kelly let out a belly laugh. It wasn't what I was going for, but it broke what little tension was left in the room, so hey, score one for me.

"That little man has a freaky bone? He looks so unassuming" Kelly mused.

"Wait." Tyler held up a hand. "When did you meet Robert Hatchett?"

"We talked to him yesterday morning, and just to be clear, I don't think he killed his wife."

Tyler shook his head. "Well, that makes two of us."

"Good," Kelly piped up from her spot in my cozy oversized armchair. "That guy is really hurting right now."

"Who *exactly* do you think killed Lydia?" I asked.

"Honestly,"—Tyler sat his mug back on the table and reached over to pet Mickey again—"I think it was your guy Jason. His money clip, jacket, and fingerprints were found at the murder scene. His alibi is shaky at best since there is no one to corroborate it, and after asking around, I think he and Lydia were in fact having an affair. All signs point to Jason King as the killer."

"But all of your evidence is circumstantial," Kelly said. "You lack a motive and proof as to whether or not the murder weapon you found is his."

"Exactly." He nodded. "But I still think he's the guy. I have some more avenues to explore, but I think they'll all lead back to Jason. Correct me if I'm wrong, but from what I understand, he isn't the most honest guy around." His gaze bore into mine, and I had to look away.

"Well, you're right about them having an affair," I said. What the hell. He'd shared his findings with me. I might as well play fair.

"What? How do you know that?" he asked.

"Jason paid a visit to my office just before I left for Trinity Grove. He admitted that they were having an affair, but with that admission aside, I still don't think he's our killer. I mean, I know Jason. He's a liar and a cheat, but there isn't a violent bone in his body," I said.

"So, Jason confirmed that they were having an affair? Why did he tell you?" Tyler asked.

"Probably because it was easier than keeping it hidden. It's not like he and I haven't had the affair discussion before."

Tyler frowned, but I ignored him.

"Seriously, I started to suspect that he and Lydia were having an affair after I found a business card with his handwriting setting up a date mixed in with the receipts that I found in Lydia's nightstand. After that, when Kelly and I questioned Robert, he told us that his wife had been leaving the house more than usual to meet old friends that she'd reconnected with on Facebook."

"He told me the same thing," Tyler said.

"But he said that after her funeral when none of her supposed friends showed up, he got curious and went online to snoop." I took a quick sip of my cocoa.

"So did I," Tyler said. "I couldn't find her on Facebook."

"Neither could Robert, but I'm sure you already know that," I said. "Robert told us that he knew immediately that she'd been lying to him, but he didn't know why. That's when he started to suspect her of having an affair, but when Jason's jacket, money clip, and fingerprints were found in their bedroom after the murder, it pretty much cinched his suspicions. So when I confronted Jason about it, he spilled the details."

"What were the receipts you found in Lydia's nightstand for?"

I readjusted my blanket. "They were for the Trinity Grove Motel. They were all dated for Friday and Saturday nights. I went to the motel last night hoping to get some answers from the night manager."

"And did you?"

Now this was where it got tricky. How much of what I found should I tell Tyler? I'd already told him more than I thought I should've if I wanted to be the one who solved this case. I knew that I should tell him everything so that he could do his job, but if I did that, I'd be allowing him to do my job too. Then where would I be? Refunding Jason's money and telling him there was nothing I could do to help him. I'd be admitting defeat, even if Tyler decided that Jason wasn't the killer, and that was something I absolutely refused to do.

But, Tyler had shared a huge piece of evidence with me and was willing to continue to do so. I owed him the truth.

Mind made up, I shrugged and forged ahead. "I talked to the night manager at the motel. She didn't like the idea of someone asking questions, but she answered the ones I asked." I rubbed the aching knot on my forehead. "She admitted that she remembered Lydia. She said Lydia almost always rented multiple rooms and that the last time she saw her, she was interested in buying a secluded cabin out by the lake."

Tyler tapped the pen he held against the small pad of paper sitting on his knee, then motioned for me to continue.

"That's what I was doing out in Trinity Grove. Mandy did a public records search and found that Lydia did in fact purchase a cabin. I headed back out to the Grove today to talk to the man who sold Lydia the cabin."

I decided to leave out the part where I'd discovered exactly what Lydia was doing in that cabin for now. That was an avenue that I wanted to pursue further. As far as I was concerned, I still had a killer to catch.

Tyler's frown deepened. "Did you learn anything from the contractor?"

"No. Just that he sold the cabin, the woman who bought it said she wanted it specifically because it was secluded, and that she had passed recently. After I left, I drove out to the cabin to check the place out. On my way home, I got turned around and didn't find my way back to the highway until it was dark."

"What did you find at the cabin?" he asked.

Although we were sharing information, I wasn't quite ready to divulge what I'd found where the cabin and Lydia's side business were concerned, so I decided to keep the gigolo business to myself for the time being.

"The gates were locked. I couldn't get in," I lied. "I looked around the outside, but there were cars in the drive, so I didn't spend much time looking around."

He frowned at me but let the subject drop.

"Did you see who ran you off of the road?" he asked.

"It was a truck. I know that from the size. Possibly dark in color, but the driver had his brights on, so I really can't be sure who was behind the wheel. I could only see a silhouette. I thought whoever was in the truck was a joyriding teenager, but when he started ramming into the back of my car, I knew I was mistaken." I shivered at the memory. "My steering wheel got stuck to the right, and I had to muscle it to stay on the road, but I was still veering to the right, and the bridge was coming up, so I had the choice of hitting the bridge head-on or steering into the culvert. The last time he slammed into me, I let go of the wheel, hit the culvert, and the car flipped. I grabbed my phone off the roof of the car where everything landed and called 9-1-1."

Tyler studied me. With every second that ticked by, the urge to squirm became almost unbearable.

"What aren't you telling me?"

I met Tyler's penetrating gaze. "What do you mean?"

He was staring at me with such intensity that I felt like I'd burst into flames if he didn't stop.

"You're leaving something out. What is it?"

My inner rebel demanded I keep my trap shut, but I ignored her. I'd intended to keep the fact that my would-be killer made a slow pass and stop to make sure the job was done to me, but Tyler was a good detective. Much better than I'd taken him for when we'd first met.

I took a deep breath, because I knew not only would this float like a lead balloon with Tyler, it was going to set Kelly off as well, since this one little fact cinched the reality that someone was actually trying to kill me.

But what choice did I have? They were both staring a hole through me, and from Tyler's expression, he wasn't taking no for an answer.

I closed my eyes and pinched the bridge of my nose for a quick second, then spilled the beans.

"After my car came to a stop on its roof, the truck that ran me off of the road turned around and drove back past me in the other direction. He slowed way down, stopped, then sped up, and left the scene."

"You were going to hide that from us?" Tyler snapped.

"I didn't want anyone to worry about me. I can take care of myself," I said.

"Barb, someone definitely wants you dead. But who?" Kelly chewed her thumbnail the way she always did when she was stressed out. By morning it would be nothing but a sore, little pink nub with a Band-Aid on it.

"That's what I'm going to find out, starting with asking Jason King where the hell he was at the time of the wreck," Tyler said as he flipped his notepad closed.

"I already told you, Jason isn't Lydia's killer, and I'm sure he wasn't the one driving the truck," I argued.

Jason could barely drive a Prius.

"Let's agree to disagree about Jason King." Tyler stood and paced. "I really wish you would drop this case, Barb. It's just too dangerous."

"Drop this case? Have you lost your mind?" I asked. "What happened to the *lets-share-information, let's-work-together* business?" I asked. "Jason paid me. I promised him I would prove his innocence, and that's what I intend to do."

"For you to prove his innocence, he has to actually *be innocent*." He ran a hand through his hair. "Refund his freaking money, and drop this case, Barb. Someone's out to kill you, and he nearly succeeded tonight. You need to take a step back and let the professionals handle this."

"Professionals?" I set my mug down on the table with a clink, and Mickey took that as his cue to find another lap to curl up on and fled. Tyler implying that I wasn't a professional raised my hackles more than nearly being killed.

"Refund his money? Drop the case? Are you crazy?" I tossed the blanket off my legs and stood. "Are you going to pay my rent? Utilities? What about my employees? They depend on this job. And what about my career?" I threw my hands in the air. "Am I supposed to drop the biggest case I've ever been given just because things have gotten a little bumpy, and it would make you feel better? Well," I pointed my finger at him. "That's just not going to happen, chief."

I was on a roll, and that was never a good thing. I tended to let my mouth write checks my behind couldn't cash when I let that happen, but Tyler had me riled up whether he'd intended to or not. My head hurt, and I was done with the night. Completely done. I wanted nothing more than a hot bubble bath and to snuggle beneath the downy linens of my bed.

Tyler stared at me as though I'd just sprouted a second head, and Kelly just sat back with a smile, enjoying the show. She was about as much help as Mickey, who'd conveniently found a new place to sit on her lap.

"Yes, I wanted to work together with you on this, but that was before you confirmed that someone was trying to kill you. Whoever ran you off of the road wouldn't have crept past the wreck unless they were trying to make sure that they'd finished the job and that you were dead. Barb, I'm worried about you," Tyler said. His brilliant green eyes blazed beneath a fringe of thick, black, mile-long lashes that I would've killed to have and frowned. "Just think about dropping the case, please."

For a split second I almost fell into his request. How easy would it be to tell Jason that I was finished? To get whoever was trying to kill me off of my back and go back to busting cheating losers? But I wasn't a quitter, and I knew that Jason was innocent.

"I'm finishing this case."

Tyler took another step toward me. "Don't test me, Barb. I will put a tail on you. Do you know what that means? It means that I'll know every little thing that you do. When you grab a burger at the corner joint. When you check your mail. Even when you use the bathroom. You won't be able to step foot outside without me being told exactly what you're doing. Exactly how much investigating do you think you'll get done then, huh?"

"Go ahead." I shrugged. "Do what you think you have to do, but I'm warning you. If you push me, I'll push back."

Now, I wasn't sure why, but standing there arguing toe-to-toe with Tyler, his muscular form towering over me, his chest and biceps straining against the thin material of his tight, black T-shirt, his jaw clenched, had me a bit hot-and-bothered.

My palms started to sweat, and I could feel the blood rushing to my cheeks, could feel the blush burning there.

Tyler stepped even closer to me, reached out, placed his finger beneath my chin, and raised my gaze to meet his. His eyes bore into mine, and a shiver slid down my spine.

"I said it once, and I'll say it again. I won't hesitate to do whatever I have to do to keep you safe, even if it means tossing your beautiful little behind in jail."

Once again I found myself standing in front of Tyler, my mouth hanging open, without a single comment, sassy or otherwise, to toss back at him.

Why did Tyler calling me beautiful send a wave of warmth swarming through me? Why did it scatter my wits like dandelion seeds on the wind?

I should be kicking and screaming to get my point through his thick head, but instead, there I stood like a big mute lump. Before I could ponder that particular question any further, Tyler turned and made his way to the door. Once there, he turned back to me.

"A patrol car will be parked across the street for the rest of the night just in case the person who ran you off of the road knows where you live and decides to make a surprise visit."

"By *the person who ran me off the road*, do you mean Jason?" I asked and crossed my arms across my chest.

Tyler glared at me and shoved the pad of paper he still held in one hand into his back pocket. "Stay inside, and I'll call you in the morning."

He didn't answer my question, probably because I already knew the answer.

"Fine."

"Kelly." He nodded in her direction, and she tossed out a salute. To my surprise, it wasn't her usual one-finger salute, which I would've preferred at the moment.

His eyes found mine once again, and I swear I saw one side of his mouth try to quirk up in a small smile. God, this man was a handful.

"Goodnight, Barb. Behave yourself."

CHAPTER EIGHT

———

The morning light peeking through the curtains of my bedroom window came way too early.

I raised my head off my pillow and frowned at the alarm clock. Nine o'clock flashed in big red numbers back at me. I flopped back down into my cozy cocoon and cringed at the tightness in my neck and the throbbing in my head.

I never slept this late, but considering the night I'd had, I didn't beat myself up too badly. I'd nearly been killed. I deserved a little rest...but only a little. I rolled over onto my back and draped my arm over my eyes. My entire body felt as though I'd been trampled by an elephant, but I guess that's to be expected after you've been in a wreck.

Kelly had stayed with me for an hour more after Tyler left. We'd watched a couple of reruns of *Three's Company*, because John Ritter was the bomb, and tried our best to put my near-death experience out of our minds, but that tension hung heavily in the air, and the question of who'd tried to kill me plagued our minds.

I hadn't told Kelly, even after Tyler left, about what I'd found at the cabin concerning Lydia's business venture. That was a huge conversation that I wanted to wait to have when all three of us were together. I was also a little afraid that if I told Kelly, she'd immediately try to make an appointment with Silas.

I tried to stretch and was greeted with a sudden throbbing in my temples. It appeared moving at all was going to be a little harder as my aching body did its best to remind me of the previous night's activities.

I was about to pry myself out of bed and get the day started when my cat jumped up beside me. He nuzzled my cheek and began purring. I wrapped my arms around his slightly obese body. Hey, he likes people food too, and who am I to deny him? I pulled him close to my chest, and he snuggled against me like he had for the last twelve years that he'd been in my life.

"What a long night, Mickey," I said as he kneaded my forearm with his front paws.

I told my BFF (best furry friend) about my night, the case, and Tyler. Talking to Mickey always seemed to help me put things into perspective, probably because he didn't offer his opinion on what I should or shouldn't do. He just listened like a good friend should. Sometimes he gave me a look, but that was as far as his opinion went.

"So, do I back off and let Detective Smarty-pants have the case, or do I keep going?"

Mickey opened one eye and gave me a *what-the-heck-do-you-think?* look.

"That's what I thought." I smiled and patted his big belly.

Mickey decided he was finished with snuggle time, stood up, and made his way to the end of the bed. He trotted around in a circle a few times, then made himself at home among the rumpled-up bedding.

I got out of bed as quickly as my sore muscles would allow and made my way to the bathroom.

I turned on the shower and while the water heated up, brushed my teeth. I couldn't stop wondering who would try to kill me. It had made for a long, mostly sleepless night. All of the clues, as limited as they were, pointed to Lydia's murderer being my would-be killer. It couldn't be simple coincidence that I had questioned Robert Hatchett, the motel night manager, Melvin, and one of Lydia's studs and then was run off the road and nearly killed.

I was missing a lot of pieces to this puzzle. Pieces I needed to solve the case, put Mr. Hatchett at ease, free Jason, and rid myself of one would-be Barb killer.

I tossed my toothbrush into the cup I always kept it in and then stepped into the shower.

I stood there and let the hot water run over my body, massaging my muscles and working out the kinks in my neck for I don't even know how long. I was exhausted, both mentally and physically. My body hurt, and my mind was still running on overdrive. Not only was I dealing with someone trying to kill me, but I had to deal with whatever was happening between Tyler and me.

There was something about that man that put me at ease and at the same time sent my nerves scattering. He was gorgeous, successful, and it was obvious that he was into me, according to Kelly anyway. Was I attracted to Tyler? Would I welcome his attentions? Yes. What sane woman wouldn't? But what did it matter? He and I would never see eye to eye about my career, not to mention it's not like he'd made any kind of move on me. Sure, he'd called me beautiful on a couple of occasions, but those were words any man could use to try to get his way. He wanted to keep me safe, but again, he was a cop. It was his job to keep everyone safe.

I washed my hair and body then stepped out of the shower and wrapped myself in a towel. I didn't have any more answers concerning Tyler and me than I did the murder case. I flipped on the blow dryer and set my hair to rights.

Mind made up, I put the idea of Tyler and me on the back burner. Whatever happened or didn't happen, I'd deal with it as it came along. For now, I had bigger fish to fry. Like how to get my purse back from the gigolo's cabin.

I still couldn't believe that I'd left my purse behind. I knew better. I was a professional for crying out loud, but here I was, acting like I hadn't been working this job for more than a few days. I wanted to kick myself. Knowing Kelly, once she heard what I'd done, she'd do the job for me.

I took a good look at myself in the mirror and cringed. The bruise that covered one side of my forehead was a dark, ugly purple/black mess. No amount of concealer and foundation would ever cover it, and I really didn't feel like putting on a full face of makeup anyway. My shoulder and chest were also a lovely shade of purple from the seat belt. But in the end, things could have been so much worse. I could totally live with a few bumps and bruises as long as I was alive.

Instead, I swiped on a coat of Flirtini lip gloss and mascara, which was generally the extent of my morning makeup routine.

Mickey had abandoned the bed and made himself at home on the floor just outside the bathroom door. I stepped over him and made my way to the closet.

I donned a pair of faded old jean shorts, a pink off the shoulder T-shirt, and slid my feet into a pair of black Converse.

I liked simple. Simple was good.

I walked to the kitchen, gave Mickey fresh food and water, and was halfway out the door before I realized that I didn't have a means of transportation.

I made a quick call to the insurance company, and they assured me that they had received my claim and that my car would be replaced, and in the meantime they would send a loaner car that would arrive within the hour. I was sure I had Tyler to thank for pushing the reports to the insurance company immediately after the accident to speed the process along. I'd find a way to thank him later. At the moment, I had more on my mind.

I settled myself at the kitchen table with the morning newspaper and called the office in hopes that Mandy would be in. Knowing her, she was already at the office.

"Jackson Investigations, this is Mandy. How may I help you?"

"It's Barb. How's everything going this morning?"

"Aren't you supposed to be resting?" she scolded me.

"I am. I'm reading the paper and drinking coffee as we speak," I said, purposely leaving out the part where I was going to be coming into the office as soon as my car arrived. I knew she meant well, but I really didn't feel like being nagged after the night I'd just had.

"Everything here is taken care of. There's nothing for you to worry about. How are you feeling?" she asked.

"I feel fine. Just a little sore," I lied. I didn't see any sense in telling Mandy that I felt as though I'd been dragged behind a truck instead of just run down with one.

"You should take it easy for a couple of days. Kelly and I can hold down the fort." I could hear the smile in her voice. She was always smiling.

"Thanks, but I need to talk to the two of you, and it's pretty important."

"Really? What?"

"I don't want to get into it too much over the phone, but I found something last night that could bust this case wide open. I'll be in as soon as my car arrives."

"Now, didn't you just say that you were going to take it easy today?" Mandy scolded me.

"No. I said I was taking it easy right at this moment. I never said it was going to last all day." I grinned and disconnected the call before she could further state her objections.

I slid the phone back into my pocket and unfolded the newspaper. I'd covered all of my bases as far as questioning suspects. Robert Hatchett, as far as I was concerned, was still as innocent as the day was long.

I hadn't been run off the road until I'd visited Trinity Grove, and that was what had my mind in a whirl. I'd spoken to Melba, the night manager of the motel, Melvin Harris, the man who had sold Lydia the cabin, and much to my surprise, a gigolo, or stud as I'd dubbed him, who worked for Lydia.

I now had a *real* list of suspects.

My stomach churned at the thought of how close I'd actually come to being killed. If whoever the culprit was who forced me off the road had taken the time to get out of the truck and see if I was actually dead, I most likely would be. I shoved the unwelcome thought to the back of my mind.

I hopped up and set my Keurig. A few minutes later I grabbed my cup of coffee and retook my seat at the kitchen table. I skimmed the newspaper to see if I'd missed anything pertaining to the case in the media but found nothing.

Lydia's case was now two weeks old, and the "new" had apparently worn off, as there wasn't a single mention of her murder.

Two cups of coffee later I was getting antsy and made my way to the living room.

I peeked out the living room window and watched as two cars pulled up alongside the curb in front of my house.

I sent a silent prayer to The Man Upstairs that the first car that had pulled up wasn't my rental car.

I opened the door and stepped out on the front porch. A tall man with the most beautiful caramel-colored skin I'd ever seen in my entire life and pale green eyes approached me.

"Good morning, ma'am. Are you Barbara Jackson?" he asked.

"Um..." I peered at the hideous monstrosity he'd hopped out of and then back at him, unsure I should tell the truth. "Yes," I said, but it came out sounding more like a question than a statement.

He smiled a brilliant white smile and handed me a digital box and plastic pen.

"Just sign here, and she's all yours."

I seriously hoped he was talking about the black Cadillac that had pulled up behind the car he'd just vacated, but I had a sinking feeling that he wasn't. My luck hadn't been the best as of late.

I signed my name and handed the box back to him. He tossed me the keys.

"Have a great day." He turned and hurried down to the car. To the black Cadillac.

I watched as it sped away then glared at the vehicle he'd left behind.

It was green, and I'm not talking about a glittery emerald green. No, it was a pea green, as big as a boat Lincoln sedan like my grandmother used to drive.

Would it have killed the insurance agency to send a car that was a little newer? Perhaps one from this century? I wasn't asking for anything fancy like an Audi or a Corvette. I drove a bright red Volkswagen Beetle for crying out loud but this? This was ridiculous.

I closed the door to my house and locked it behind me.

I didn't have time to complain about the atrocity of the car I was stuck driving for the next two weeks. I had an investigation to wrap up. Not that I'd be very inconspicuous in the pea-soup wagon. I'd stick out like a sore thumb everywhere I went in that thing, but at the moment I didn't have a choice.

I opened the door and slid into the driver seat. The interior wasn't much more attractive than the exterior. The seats were a pale ivory vinyl, and the dashboard was a horrible faux wood-grain panel. I started the car, cringed at a squealing belt beneath the hood, and pulled away from the curb. I flicked on the air conditioner, but all I got in return was a loud squeal and rattle, and then a burst of dust exploded from the vents. I coughed and sputtered as I tried to navigate the car down the street and wave the dust out of my face at the same time.

Great. I was cruising around in a pea-green sedan with vinyl seats. It was inching upward of ninety degrees, and the air conditioner didn't work. I could feel the heat of the hot vinyl seat through my jeans.

After this case was over, I was seriously considering taking Kelly's advice and going on a long-overdue vacation.

In the last forty-eight hours I'd questioned a widower, a lying, cheating ex-boyfriend, a shifty motel manager, a construction worker, and a gigolo. I'd been run off the road and left for dead, not to mention I was dealing with a hunky detective who sort of acted like he might possibly have a little attraction to me.

I took a deep breath and pressed my foot down on the accelerator, then rolled down all of the windows in an attempt to let the dust dissipate. I steered the car toward the office. What I wouldn't give to have my little car back, I thought as the wind blew a stray hair that had come loose from my ponytail into my mouth, and I struggled to spit it out.

This day couldn't possibly get any worse...could it?

CHAPTER NINE

———

"She was a freaking pimp? Like a real-life, selling-some-man-booty pimp?"

"I think the correct term is madam," Mandy corrected.

"No, that can't be right. I thought a madam only applied if you were pimping women?"

"I don't think so. I think it works both ways." Mandy scrunched her nose. "I'm not sure. Isn't a pimp a man?"

I shook my head and immediately regretted the action as my brain pounded against my skull in protest. I reached into my desk drawer and pulled out an individual packet of Ibuprofen. While Kelly and Mandy debated what Lydia's proper title should be, I popped the pills into my mouth and chased them down with another much-needed coffee.

"As amusing as all of that is, it's beside the point." I held up a hand. "How in the hell could I have left my purse at that house? What am I? Some kind of amateur? What if one of those guys was the one who tried to kill me? What if one of them killed Lydia? Now they know where this office is and where I live. The killer could come after all of us."

I hung my head in my hands. What in the hell had I been thinking? The truth was, I hadn't been. I'd been so shocked by my little stud-farm discovery that I'd done the one thing I knew better than to ever do. I lost my cool.

"You don't need to worry about any of that. We won't hurt you…or I won't anyway. You didn't have to lie about who you really are though."

We all three looked up and spotted Silas standing just inside my office doorway looking every inch a sex god.

"I can explain." I stood and made my way around the desk.

"No need," he said. Then he approached me. He practically pressed his chest against mine as he leaned forward and set my purse gently atop the desk. His scent was a heady blend of spice and vanilla, and for a moment I wanted to lean in and inhale deeply. He must've known what I was thinking because he smiled down at me mischievously and then stepped back slowly.

"Now that I know who and what you are and why you left the house so quickly, I think I know exactly what you were doing at the house in the first place. I want to help."

He wanted to help? At this point I'd take any help I could get, even if that help came in the form of a six-foot-tall gigolo. I wasn't into objectifying men, but even if he couldn't give us any information that would help the case, he would at least serve as an excellent piece of eye candy.

"In that case, have a seat." I motioned to the chairs situated before my desk then to the girls. "This is Kelly and Mandy, my associates. Ladies, this is Silas…"

"Thorne." He smiled. "Silas Thorne."

Mandy and Kelly sat still in their chairs, their mouths gaping open, and if I wasn't mistaken, a little drool came from the corners of their lips.

"Can we get you anything, Mr. Thorne?" I asked as I retook my seat.

He grinned that devastating grin of his. "I think after what we shared back at the cabin we can dispense with the formalities, don't you? You can call me Silas."

I felt a hot blush stain my cheeks at his words. Kelly and Mandy moved their gawking expressions to me. They didn't help matters any, and I felt my cheeks growing redder. Sometimes I wondered how on Earth I even pretended to be professional.

"What exactly happened between the two of you at the cabin?"

I jerked my gaze to the doorway and to my horror found Tyler staring at me with a look so demanding I felt myself shiver under its scrutiny.

"Didn't I teach either of you two to lock the freaking door?" I snapped, but the girls just shrugged and grinned at my distress. I pressed the palm of my hand to my forehead, careful to avoid the knot and bruise still residing there.

"What happened at the cabin?" Tyler asked again, the growl more evident in his voice this time around.

If I hadn't known any better, I would have mistaken his reaction as one born of jealousy. But that couldn't be what I was hearing. Tyler and I hadn't even shared, well, anything even remotely intimate in my estimation. We barely knew each other.

"Nothing happened between us at the cabin, not that it's any of anyone's business." I reached into my top desk drawer, pulled out a piece of gum, and popped it into my mouth.

Nervous habit. Had I been close to the coffeepot I'd have been drinking straight from the carafe.

"Just a kiss," Silas said with a smile. "Her lips are so full, the kind that always seem to be begging for a kiss. Wouldn't you agree?"

Silas was a charming, flirtatious man, but I guessed one would have to be in his line of work. Nothing seemed to bother him, as evidenced by the way he continued to grin at me even though Tyler looked fit to kill.

"A kiss?" Tyler growled and strode to the edge of my desk. He balled up his fists and leaned onto his knuckles against the desktop. He glared at me.

Kelly and Mandy were obviously still enjoying the show. They wore matching grins as they glanced between the two men and me. I was surprised they hadn't made popcorn and settled in for the show.

Tickets to watch Barb's distress: $5.99.

I couldn't figure out why Tyler was getting all fired up over me having been kissed by another man? It wasn't like he'd called dibs on me or anything.

I shook my head and closed my eyes.

"It was a misunderstanding." I defended myself. Even though there was absolutely zero reason for me to do so, I still felt the need to explain.

"Is there something you wanted, Tyler? I'm with a client."

"I can wait," he grumbled and crossed his arms over his chest.

His alpha-male attitude just wasn't doing it for me at the moment. I'd had a long night, and the morning wasn't shaping up to be much better, so I pointed toward the door. "Then wait outside."

His glare intensified, but after a moment he relented and took a step away from the desk. He snarled down at Silas, where the moron sat still grinning like an idiot, then turned toward my office door.

Mandy and Kelly stood up with much less vigor than usual and escorted Tyler from the room. Apparently they didn't like the idea of missing the show but had a job to do.

Once the girls and Tyler had left the room and closed the door firmly behind them, I addressed Silas.

"Thank you for returning my purse."

"You're most welcome." He frowned and leaned forward. "What happened to you? Where'd you get that bruise?" he motioned to the purple knot on my forehead.

When I'd touched my forehead earlier, I must've moved my hair enough to expose the bruise.

"I had a little car accident on my way home from your place last night." I watched his expression for any change in his reaction to my revelation. Anything that might convey that he wasn't shocked by the news. He appeared genuinely surprised and a bit concerned.

Call me crazy, but I had a feeling that Silas wasn't the person who'd run me off the road.

"Are you all right?" he asked.

"Just a little headache. Thanks for asking."

He leaned back in the chair and laced his fingers together. "I don't like to see women hurt. I'm glad you're all right."

"Thank you. Really." I smiled at his kindness.

"Other than my returning your purse, I bet you're wondering exactly why I'm here," he said.

"I am," I admitted and leaned back in my chair. "You said you wanted to help. What exactly do you think it is that I need help with?"

"You're looking for Lydia's killer."

I wasn't surprised that he knew why I'd stopped by the cabin. He worked for Lydia, knew she'd been murdered, so it made sense that when a private investigator paid a visit, it would have to do with Lydia's demise.

I nodded. "Go on."

He rubbed his fingertip across his chin. "What do you want to know?"

"Everything," I said honestly. "How about you start with how you came to be a gigolo under Lydia's management?" I wasn't about to tell the cheeky man that I'd dubbed them studs. I could only imagine the fun he'd have at my expense over that one.

"It just kind of happened, really." He shrugged. "I filled in for a friend as a waiter at one of Lydia's charity events one night. She slipped her number into my jacket pocket and told me to call her, that she had a job opportunity I might be interested in. Of course I called her. I'm in art school, and waiting tables and working parties doesn't pay the bills or tuition."

"And she just offered you the position of gigolo, and you went along with it? Just like that? *Hey, how'd you like to sell your body for money?*"

I had a hard time believing she just popped the offer out there right off the bat, but what did I know? This was my first run-in with the sex trade.

"No." He laughed. "She sat me down and eased me into it. She explained the offer to me in detail. Basically, I run the show and get paid for it. She explained what the job entailed, that I could choose clients, what my hard limits were, what I could charge, that I could choose the hours I wanted to work and so on, and I'd be making more money in a week than in an entire month as a waiter."

Not that I would ever consider becoming a hooker, but the perks Silas listed would be hard for anyone to turn down.

"And sex with random women. No strings attached, all fun, all the time," I added. "That had to be a major deciding factor, didn't it? A young, virile man such as yourself had to see that as a perk."

He shook his head. "It isn't all about the sex." He leaned forward and met my gaze. "Yes, we have sex with women, but it's more than that. It's about making them feel like queens. Women don't just come to us for a ride and then prance back off to their home and normal everyday lives like nothing happened. They come to us looking for an experience. To be treated like the only woman in the world. To be cherished if only for that hour or for that night. Sex is simply the end result and where they wish to be cherished the most in that moment. "

I understood. Really, I did. How many women out there felt stuck in a rut? How many felt ordinary? Lydia had tapped into a market that would make her a fortune.

"I understand." And really, I did. "Was your relationship with Lydia strictly professional?"

He leaned back in his chair and laced his fingers behind his head. "If you're asking if we had sex, then the answer is yes but only once. When she hired me. She said she needed to see how well I performed before putting me to work. Apparently I passed her audition because I was put in the book and had appointments the very next day and every day since."

"So, Lydia had sex with every man she hired?"

"As far as I know, yes." He nodded. "But per her rules, there was to never be a repeat performance. After the audition we were to keep our relationship strictly professional, and that suited me just fine. I liked Lydia. She gave me a job that more than pays my bills and a place to live, but I wasn't interested in or attracted to her romantically."

"How many of you are there? Gigolos living in the house, I mean."

"Four." He shrugged. "I was the second man she hired. Max was the first. We worked out of the motel for a few months until we'd made Lydia enough money to buy the cabin. You see," he said, "she used small amounts of her husband's money to rent the motel. A couple of hundred here and there wouldn't raise eyebrows, but a large sum, say, enough to purchase a cabin, would have. Then she'd have questions to answer, and everything she'd built would fall apart."

"I see. So what happens now that she's dead?"

"After she passed, the cabin went to us, and now we four own it."

"I'm lost." I held up a hand. "How did the cabin go to you? When her will was read, everything went to her husband."

Of course, there was no mention of the cabin or Lydia's little side business in said will either.

"She had a second will and attorney in Trinity Grove. Everything pertaining to the business was dealt with in that separate will. She kept the entire business based in the Grove so that there was no chance of it colliding with anything she and her husband had going on in the city," he explained. "The cabin was willed over to the four of us, Max, Chase, Billy, and me, to do with as we saw fit, and the money she'd made off us was divided and given back to us. We decided to keep the business going with our regular clients. We'll add a few more clients here and there as our regulars sometimes tell their friends about us if we give them permission to do so."

"Did you know of anyone who wanted to harm Lydia?"

He shook his head. "Lydia was a wonderful person. Always happy, always wanting to help someone. I can't imagine anyone wanting to kill her. But they did, didn't they?" He shook his head, and for a moment I was mesmerized by his perfectly blond hair and sharp profile. What did he have to do to achieve that perfect color? Sell his soul? He had to have made some kind of deal with the devil to look as tasty as he did. I shook myself away from my wayward thoughts.

"What about someone who liked Lydia? Maybe someone who liked her a little too much?"

I thought that perhaps I was looking in the wrong direction. Maybe I should've been concentrating on someone Lydia was having an affair with other than Jason, rather than someone who hated her.

"She was having an affair with her accountant Jason King. We all knew about it. She trusted us, and we trusted her, but I don't think he killed her." He frowned. "There was no one else that I'm aware of."

I didn't think so either. So where did that leave me? Disgruntled husbands maybe?

"How many regulars do each of you have?"

He chuckled and blew out a breath. "Ten. Fifteen. Some of us have more. Some have less."

If each man had fifteen regulars that meant there were sixty possibly disgruntled husbands out there who could've wanted Lydia dead because she'd set their wives up with other men. I already knew there was no way on earth that Silas and the others would give up the names of their regulars, so I didn't even bother asking.

That was it. I was at a dead end.

"I'm sorry to cut this short, but I have to be going. I do hope you find Lydia's killer. She was a good woman."

"I'll do my best," I promised.

Silas and I stood. I rounded the desk and came to a stop before him. I offered my hand for a handshake.

"I appreciate all of your help. If you remember anything that might help me with this case, please don't hesitate to call. I'm going to be honest with you." I looked him in the eyes. "I need all of the help I can get at this point."

He glanced down at my outstretched hand, then back at my face. His glittering blue eyes flashed mischievously, and before I knew what he was about, he pulled me into his arms and once again kissed me senseless.

It was a quick but still lava-hot kiss.

After he broke the kiss, he raised his head and grinned down at me. "Your boyfriend isn't going to be too happy about that." He tilted his head toward the office door. "But I really couldn't care less. It was worth it."

Before I could correct Silas that Tyler wasn't my boyfriend, he set me away from him then made his way to the door. With a perfect swagger in his step, he strode out of my office all the while wearing a grin the size of the Grand Canyon.

Before I could fully compose myself, Tyler came stomping into my office and slammed the door behind him, cutting off Kelly's fast approach.

"What in the living hell was that all about? You let him kiss you? You don't even know that guy. What were you thinking? *Were* you even thinking?"

I calmly leaned my bum against my desk, crossed my arms over my chest, and tried to ignore my still-throbbing lips. I'm not going to lie, that kiss had been *good*.

"My, my, my, Detective Black, if I didn't know any better I'd say that you're more upset by that fact that an extremely attractive man kissed me than you are by the fact that I was nearly killed last night."

He stepped closer to me and completely invaded my personal space, but honestly, it kind of felt good.

"I'm not jealous, especially not over that cover-model wannabe."

"He looked like a little more than a wannabe to me." I tilted my head and grinned.

He clenched his jaw. I saw the vein in his neck pulsate, and I instantly stood a little straighter. Not because I feared him, but because I secretly wished *he'd* kiss me. I don't know why, but in that moment I wanted to feel those lips that were frowning at me on mine.

"He might be attractive, might make your heart beat a little quicker." He snaked one big, strong arm around my waist and pulled me tight against his body, then slid his other hand behind my head where he pulled the elastic tie from my hair and threaded his fingers through its now-loose tresses. "But he's not what you need."

I'm not sure what I expected Tyler's kiss to be like, but I'm certain I couldn't have imagined it any better.

His lips were firm yet soft. Commanding yet gentle. His fingers tightened in my hair at the same time his arm did around my waist. He pulled me tighter against him. I melted into his embrace and relished his attentions.

The kisses I'd shared with Silas had been hot, toe-curling even, but they had *nothing* on what was happening to me while in Tyler's strong arms.

This wasn't a good thing, Tyler kissing me, and yet I couldn't come up with a reason why I should make him stop. Was there really a good reason? We were both grown adults. We were able to make our own decisions.

The kiss ended, and instead of setting me aside as Silas had done, Tyler held me close and peered down into my eyes.

"I don't want you to get hurt again, Barb."

I grinned up at him like an idiot. Because at the moment, I felt like a teenage girl being swept away by the quarterback of the high school football team.

"Because you lliiikkke me?" I said in a singsong voice. Call me crazy, but the thought of being a little more than friends with the good detective suited me just fine.

"Maybe a little." He chuckled then became serious once again. "I know that this is your job, but promise me you won't do anything overly dangerous. Go home tonight and stay there. If you have to snoop around, take one of the girls with you, and call me, please. I can't do my job if I'm too busy worrying about you."

"You worry about me?" I smiled.

He grinned and shook his head like he couldn't believe my antics or whatever it was that he was feeling for me.

"I'm tired of fighting it, Barb. As insane as it may be, I like you...a lot," he admitted and smoothed a strand of hair behind my ear.

I'd never checked in with a man in my entire life, but something about the way Tyler asked, the way he was looking at me, had me nodding my head in agreement.

He was a detective. I'd be wise to listen to his judgment once in a while.

"I know you won't tell me about anything you've found since our talk last night, so I'm not even going to ask, but I will ask this, do you have plans to do any sneaking around tonight?"

"Unfortunately, no." I shook my head. "I plan on going home, taking a hot bath, eating leftover pizza, and watching a movie. An extremely cheesy action flick, if I can manage it."

"Would you like some company? I'll bring fresh pizza *and* beer?"

Even though his proposal sounded like heaven to a homebody like me, I had to get one thing straight first.

"What is this?" I motioned between us. "I just... I need to have some idea of what's going on between us."

I was a simple girl with simple needs, and one of those simple needs was the need to know exactly what was or wasn't happening between me and the man standing across from me.

He shook his head, ran his fingers through his thick, black hair, and then blew out a breath. "Honestly, I don't know, Barb. All I know is that I like you, I'm attracted to you, and I don't want you to get hurt. I want to get to know you better. On a personal level."

That was as good an explanation as any that I could give at the present moment should he have asked me the same question. Despite how handsome the doctor had been, and how insanely hot Silas was, they just didn't top Tyler. I liked him, found myself thinking about him at the most inopportune times, and he was genuine.

I smiled. "Good. In that case, you're on, but only if you promise you won't forget the beer. I could really use one right about now."

"I promise. How's eight o'clock?"

"Perfect," I said.

He kissed me quickly on the lips then hurried out of my office as though he was afraid I'd change my mind if he stuck around any longer.

Once Tyler was gone, Kelly and Mandy stuck their heads around the doorframe and grinned. Kelly shook her finger at me. "A sex-god gigolo *and* a hunky detective all in one day? Someone's been a busy girl."

CHAPTER TEN

———

Once the alpha males had left the office, I'd lost track of time while catching up with clients over the phone about now-closed and ongoing investigations. I finally left the office around seven-thirty. Mandy and Kelly had called it quits shortly after six o'clock.

After the events of the past twenty-four hours, the ten-minute drive to my small house on the outskirts of town felt more like an hour.

The neighborhood was quiet, small, and filled with mostly retired couples and newlyweds just starting on their marital adventure. All in all, it was paradise for an outgoing introvert such as me.

I'd be lying if I said that there weren't times when I felt a bit out of place being the only person in the neighborhood who was still single, who worked all hours of the day and night, and had zero kids, unless you counted my cat Mickey, which most people didn't.

But everyone was always polite, and my neighbor, Mrs. Grady, brought over a tamale casserole every Wednesday night in exchange for me helping her with her crossword puzzle. So it all evened itself out in the end I suppose.

I pulled the green eyesore into the driveway, killed the ignition, and made my way up the pathway leading to my front door, jangling my keys the entire way. The porch light was off, which I found odd, as it was solar-activated and came on automatically when the sun started to set, but as tired as I was, I didn't give it a second thought.

I climbed the three short steps up to my porch and reached for the doorknob, but when my fingertips touched the knob, the door rocked open an inch.

I always locked my doors, not just for my safety but for Mickey's as well.

The grogginess I'd had disappeared.

Nothing like the possibility of a murdering intruder to wake a person up.

I reached behind me, pulled my gun from the waistband of my jeans, and then slipped silently into my house. With my back pressed against the wall, I looked around cautiously.

Nothing appeared out of place.

My main concern wasn't really for my belongings, but for my cat. Where in the world was he? Was he all right?

On silent feet, I eased deeper into the house, careful to keep my back pressed against the wall every step as I made my way toward the bedroom. The guest bathroom door stood open. I peeked in and found it in the same shape I'd left it in. I eased on down the short hallway to my bedroom, keeping my eyes peeled for Mickey the entire time. I stepped into the room quickly with my gun thrust out before me. Much to my surprise, it too was in the same shape I'd left it in...with the exception of the bathroom door.

It was shut tight. I always left the bathroom door open because Mickey liked to sometimes sleep on the closed toilet seat. He liked the fuzzy cover Mona had insisted I put on the lid when I'd moved in.

My ancient cat could be a bit goofy at times, but I loved him all the same.

I crept my way to the door, pressed my back to the wall beside it, counted to three, then flung the bathroom door open, and stepped into the doorway with my gun drawn.

Mickey came bounding out of the bathroom so hard and fast he slammed into my legs. I lost my grip on the gun, and it fell to the floor as I stumbled backward, arms flailing in the air reaching for purchase

I fell into a hard body. I turned, fully expecting to see Tyler, but I saw the butt of a pistol slamming into my temple instead.

CHAPTER ELEVEN

———

My head pounded like a speaker at a heavy-metal concert.

I wanted to open my eyes, to look around and see where I was, but my lids felt like they weighed fifty pounds each and just wouldn't cooperate. I tried to reach up and rub them, but my arms were already above my head. That's when I realized that my hands were bound, as were my feet.

Panic shot through me. I pried my lids open. They felt gritty, like the backs of my eyelids were made of sandpaper. I struggled to focus. I looked through blurry eyes at the ropes twisted around my wrists. My hands were tied in front of me and connected to a rope that looked to be about a foot long. The rest of the rope was looped around a bedpost at the foot of the bed. The binding was surprisingly soft but still incredibly tight. I tested my bonds, but they held firm. Someone obviously knew how to work a rope.

A terrible taste sat heavily in my mouth, and my head swam. I felt drunk, and my stomach rolled with nausea, I'd either been drugged or had one heck of a concussion.

I took deep, cleansing breaths hoping to rid myself of the groggy feeling and gather my wits. I was in one heck of a situation with no idea how I'd ended up there in the first place.

A soft grunt sounded to the left of me. I forced my stiff neck to turn in the direction of the sound and gaped at what I found.

"Silas? Jason? What in the hell?"

Silas was tied like me to the opposite bedpost at the foot of the bed. I glanced around and spotted Jason tied up on the floor in front of the dresser.

I blinked in an attempt to clear my blurry vision and continued my deep breathing. Jason was out cold, but Silas was groaning and slumped to the side toward me. I scooted my bottom as far as I could in Silas's direction, then reached out and kicked him once, twice, a third time.

"Darn it, knock it off!" he growled then craned his neck to look at me. "Barb?"

I hadn't meant to kick him in the head, but I didn't have time to worry about the pained, accusing look he finally directed toward me. He was awake, and two heads were better than one. Jason was too far away, and he was hog-tied instead of leashed to the bedposts as Silas and I were.

"What are you doing? Where are we? What happened?" he asked as he struggled to sit up. He blinked his eyes and leaned his head back against the post. He pulled at the binding on his hands and cursed. "What in the hell is going on?"

"I don't know," I said and glanced around the bedroom. "We're obviously in a bedroom, but I don't know whose, where, or why."

Silas looked around and then frowned.

"I know where we are."

"Where?" I asked.

"We're at the cabin. This is Lydia's room. The master bedroom. Max's bedroom now."

"Lydia's room?"

"Auditions," he simply said.

I knew what he meant from our previous conversation.

"If we're at your cabin, where is everyone? Why haven't we been found? Surely someone would notice you being dragged into this room and Jason and I being carried in."

"This is mine and Max's day off." Silas frowned. "He's visiting his mother in Vegas. Billy and Chase were booked for overnights with clients. They won't be back until Sunday morning."

"Why do you know each other's schedules?"

"It's safer for each of us to know where the others are. What would happen if a crazed husband or boyfriend attacked us or killed us, and no one knew our last whereabouts or who we were with?"

"That makes sense."

"And we're friends. We talk to each other, you know. I'm sure you tell your girls where you're going. You discuss vacations, jobs, and such. Am I right?" he asked.

I nodded and immediately regretted the action. My stomach rolled, and my head throbbed.

Breathe. Just breathe, I told myself.

"So, it looks like we're on our own," I said.

"Looks like it," Silas answered. "What's the last thing you remember?"

I thought back as bleary memories slowly returned to me. "I left the office late and had just gotten home. The door was unlocked." I thought back. "Someone broke into my house. I was searching the place when someone hit me in the head. Next thing I know, I woke up here," I said.

Silas nodded. "I left your office, came home, and then went into my bedroom. I was about to shower when the same thing happened to me."

That explained why he was wearing only a pair of tight, spandex-like boxer briefs that left little in the package area to the imagination. Had we not been in a dire situation, I might have taken a moment to enjoy the view.

"Someone hit me over the head," he continued, "and that's all that I remember until you decided to kick me in the head and remind me how badly it hurts."

"Sorry about that."

I looked over at Jason. "We need to wake him up and figure out a way to get the heck out of here. Maybe he knows who took us."

"I'll do it. I'm closer to him," Silas volunteered. I swear I saw the corner of his mouth tick up mischievously.

Silas scooted as far away from the bedpost as he could then kicked out with his foot. I almost smiled when the ball of his foot collided with the side of Jason's head.

I didn't feel as bad about Jason being smacked in the head as I did when I'd kicked Silas. I guess a part of me still resented Jason's treatment of me when we were together and his lying about his involvement with Lydia.

Silas kicked Jason three more times before he finally groaned and glared up at him.

"Why in the hell are you kicking me? Stop it," he snapped. "Where am I?" He looked around with confusion, and then he spotted me. "Barb? What's going on? Are you hurt?"

I shook my head. "I don't think so. My head hurts, and I feel like I've been hit by a truck. Other than that, I'm fine. Do you know how you got here? Did you see who took you?" I asked.

Jason couldn't sit up because of the way he was tied with his hands and feet connected by a rope behind his back, so he just lay there like a lump and told his story.

"I'd just gotten home from the office," he began with a frown. "I stepped into the kitchen to make some coffee. Then someone hit me, and everything went black. The next thing I know, I'm waking up to that Ken doll kicking me in the head." He glared again at Silas.

Silas actually grinned.

I'd come to the conclusion that nothing fazed that gorgeous man.

I liked him.

"We need to get the heck out of here before whoever took us comes back." I stood up on shaky legs and looked around the room for something to cut away the ropes with. The dresser was too far away to even consider searching for anything of use there. The same went for the side tables next to the window and door. That left the nightstand, if I could actually reach it. I had about a foot of rope between the bedpost and me, which meant I had about a foot of freedom.

I sat down facing the post and scooted as far away as I could. Once my arms were extended before me and the rope was pulled tight, I stretched my leg out behind me. My toe barely reached the handle of the nightstand. With the toe of my shoe I attempted to pull the handle. The drawer slipped out a measly inch. It was times like these when I wished I'd been blessed with a little more height. Five measly feet didn't get you far in times like these.

"What are you doing?" Jason asked from his prone position on the floor.

"She's looking for something to cut the ropes with and free us, genius." Silas answered Jason's question, then started doing the same thing I was only on the other nightstand.

His drawer, however, came out on the first try thanks to his long, muscular legs.

I admit I stopped and watched him work.

"Oh, God..." Jason groaned in my direction. "We're about to die, and you're ogling Mr. GQ? Really, Barb?"

Silas grinned at me and flexed his abs.

I'd come to the conclusion that we were both crazy because I simply smiled and shrugged then went back to work on getting the drawer open.

I gave the drawer one last yank, if you could call it that, with the toe of my Chuck Taylor sneaker. The drawer finally fell out and hit the floor.

"Did you find anything useful?" Silas asked.

I blew out a sigh and rooted around the contents of the drawer with my foot. "I got a mini bottle of Jack, some lube, and a copy of *Busty MILF's IV*." I raised an eyebrow with surprise. "Huh, I guess that DVD *was* hers." I shrugged the best I could. "Go figure."

Silas laughed. "Lydia was bisexual. Our little secret. Not that it matters now."

"That's all well and good," I said, "but there's nothing in here that we can use to cut these ropes."

"That's good, because we wouldn't want you to get free now, would we?"

The three of us froze in place as the same handsome face I'd seen peeking at Silas and me over the balcony the day before stared at us from the now-open bedroom door.

"Max?" Silas frowned. "What's going on? Untie us."

Max shook his head. "I'm afraid I can't do that."

"Why the hell not?" Silas asked.

"Yeah, why the hell not?" I mean, I was really lost on this one. Why would a gigolo I'd never met want to kill me, Jason, or his friend for that matter?

Max stepped deeper into the room and kicked the door shut behind him. His closely cropped hair was slightly damp. He wore a pair of faded old jeans, a T-shirt, and boots. He was pretty hot, for a psycho that is.

"Because, pretty lady"—his Latino accent was thick as he spoke to me—"you're poking your nose into my business, and I can't let you continue down that road. Too many bumps, if you know what I mean."

"I really don't." I shook my head.

"That makes two of us," Silas agreed. "Why are we here?"

"Does this have something to do with Lydia?" I asked.

Max stared at me with an unreadable expression.

I instantly knew why we were tied up in the room. "You killed Lydia, didn't you?"

Max sighed dramatically. "Lydia killed herself by hooking up with him." Max pointed at Jason where he lay on the floor.

"What? I don't get it, Max. Why?" Silas asked.

"Lydia and I started this business together." Max leaned his back against the door "I was her first hire. Then you came along, then the others." He shrugged. "I was fine with her sleeping with the three of you. It was business. She needed to know that you were good at what you do. You had your one time then moved on. Then he came along." Max reached out and kicked Jason square in the face.

I cringed at the sound of his nose snapping beneath Max's heel. The sound was sickening, and my already queasy stomach roiled in protest. I took a deep breath and gathered my composure.

Jason went out like a light. Blood pooled from his surely broken nose beneath his face on the carpet.

"You and Lydia were having an affair?" I asked.

"Correct again, pretty lady." He looked at me.

Despite the pain in my head, I rolled my eyes. He seriously needed to stop with the *pretty lady* business. It was getting old real fast.

"We never stopped," he continued. "Lydia and I had something special…or so I thought. Then she took up with this maggot and told me we needed to scale our relationship back to strictly professional."

"What about her husband?"

Call me strange, but I thought Max would be a little more upset by the fact that Lydia wouldn't leave her husband rather than her taking on another lover.

"She told me she was going to leave him, but after she started sleeping with that," he nodded in Jason's direction, "I think she tossed that idea aside, like she did me. With him, she could keep her husband and live the best of both worlds. Have her cake and eat it too, I guess you would say."

The look in his eyes darkened as he glared down at Jason's prone form.

"But why kill us?" I tried to keep him talking. "I understand Jason, but why me? Why Silas?"

"Because you were getting too close. If I let you continue poking around you'd discover that I'd killed Lydia, and I couldn't allow that."

"But how? How did you know I was getting too close?"

Max smiled. "Melba."

"Melba?"

"That's right. She called me right after you paid her a visit about the receipts. She told me there was a private investigator asking questions about Lydia."

"I take it that Melba is one of your clients. Why else would she tell you about my visit? Did she know you killed Lydia?"

"No." Max shook his head. "She was only afraid that we'd be found out, and this place would be shut down. If that happened, where would she get her Friday night tumble between the sheets?"

I struggled to stifle a shudder as the image of Melba tumbling around between the sheets slithered unwelcome through my mind.

That was definitely an image I'd never be able to forget.

"As for Silas"—he sighed—"well, he sealed his fate when he visited your office. I knew he would offer any assistance that he could to help you catch Lydia's killer. He might not have been intimate with her, but they were still friends."

"How'd you get us here without someone seeing you?"

My neighbors were old and crotchety, but I was sure they would've seen the problem with someone shoving a limp body into a car and reported it.

"Silas was easy, as he was already here. You and that one"—he kicked Jason again—"were a little trickier. I snuck into your house, cracked you on the head, and then gave you a little something to keep you unconscious on the ride here. Your neighborhood is quiet, and it was dark. No one saw me toss your little behind into the backseat. It was really quite easy." He shrugged.

"Max, buddy, you've gone insane," Silas said and shook his head. "You're going to kill us? Then what? How do you plan on getting away with it?"

Max laughed. "The same way I got away with killing Lydia. I'll pin it on this guy." He walked over and kicked Jason with the toe of his shoe. "I'll say he broke in, killed the two of you while you were...indisposed." He waggled his eyebrows. "I'll say that I heard the gunshots, came running in, and saw him with a gun and your bodies dead on the bed. I'll say he attacked me, and I shot him in self-defense during the struggle."

He had everything all figured out while I was still struggling with the fact that he was doing all of this because the married woman he was having an affair with broke up with him. People were crazy.

"Wait," I said. "Why kill Lydia? Why didn't you just kill Jason?"

Max arched an eyebrow. "That was the original plan. I was going to overdose him with the drug that I gave you all to get you here. I told Lydia my plan. I admit it wasn't the brightest idea, and I'm not even sure why I told her what I'd planned to do. She asked me to come over so we could talk. She said she wanted to be with me, so I paid Lydia a visit at her home in the city. When I got there, she invited me into the bedroom."

His expression darkened. "When I moved in to kiss her, she pulled a gun on me. She thought she could threaten me, and I would back off. I knew then that she never cared about me. Things got out of hand, and I killed her."

He stared off into space for a few seconds.

He was crazy. Or as Kelly would say, his cheese had officially slid off his cracker.

He snapped back to reality and clapped his hands together.

"So, let's get this show on the road before he wakes up." Max pulled a gun from the waist of his jeans and aimed it at Silas. "I can't shoot you where you sit, or the cops will know what really happened, so this is what we're going to do. I'm going to cut you loose from the post, and you're going to hop on the bed, and you're not going to cause a fuss, or I'll blow your head off and tell the cops you tried to fight with Jason too, but he killed you before I could intervene. Understand?"

"Yeah, I get it."

"You just sit there and be a good girl." Max winked at me. "I'll get to you in a minute."

Even in the process of murder the guy couldn't turn off his gigolo charm.

I rolled my eyes.

Max held the gun on Silas as he approached him, then reached into his pocket and pulled out a small pocketknife. He opened the blade and sliced through the rope securing Silas to the bedpost. Max then slid the knife back into his front pocket.

Instead of Silas being a good boy as Max had instructed, he drew back as far as he could and hammered Max in the side of the head with his fist.

Seriously, who thought obviously naughty Silas was capable of being a good boy?

Max dropped the knife but kept a firm grip on the gun as he stumbled and fell to the floor. Before he could get his bearings, Silas was on him, holding the arm gripping the gun to the floor. Max fought back, striking Silas in the head with his one free fist.

Silas pounded Max's hand holding the gun on the floor. The pistol finally flew from Max's hands and landed next to Jason's limp body. I stretched as far as I could but still couldn't reach the gun.

Max flipped over onto Silas and started punching him in the head and face, but Silas wasn't a slouch and was giving Max a run for his money.

Jason was as useless as ever, still knocked out cold from Max's boot to the face. I looked around frantically in search of anything that could help me free myself and help Silas. My gaze landed on Lydia's porn DVD.

I stretched my leg out again and pulled the DVD to me with the toe of my shoe. I tried to pry open the case with my feet. After what felt like forever, the plastic case finally popped open. I stomped on the DVD until it broke it in half. I used my feet to scoot a broken piece up to the post then wiggled my bound hands down toward the floor as far as I could.

I worked the broken piece of DVD up the bedpost with my foot. I almost wept with joy when the shard reached my fingertips, and I was able to grip it in my hands.

There was no time to waste. I glanced to where Max and Silas were still pummeling each other, but Max had gotten in a hard shot to the side of Silas's head, and he looked like he was seconds away from going unconscious.

I sawed at the ropes binding my hands with the flimsy plastic. I was halfway through the rope when I saw Max kick Silas to the side and scramble for the gun.

A shot ripped through the air at the same time the DVD sawed through the last thread of rope around my wrists. I saw the bullet rip through Silas's shoulder. The force of the bullet hitting him flung him backward. He fell, hitting his head against the window frame on his way down.

He was out cold, and I was now on my own.

I sprang to my feet and pounced on Max. He was still on his knees, so I kicked him in the face as hard as I could. The gun flew out of his hands and landed beside Silas. I did what I knew would immobilize him. I kicked him as hard as I could in his well-paid man-bits. He squealed and rolled up into a tight ball.

I lunged for the gun. He saw what I was doing and jumped to his feet. I grabbed the gun and turned just as he leaped to throw himself on top of me.

I fired.

His body flung to the side and fell to the floor in a crumpled heap.

And suddenly everything was still.

I felt my heart beating in my chest, could almost hear it as I stared at the man I was certain I'd just killed. I'd never killed anyone before, only maimed. It was a strange, empty feeling. In that moment I thought about Tyler.

His job was much harder than I ever realized.

I got to my feet slowly and made my way over to Silas. I ripped off a piece of my T-shirt and tied it around his bleeding shoulder the best I could, then turned his head toward me and tapped his cheek. He blinked up at me.

"Are you all right?"

"I think so. Are you?"

I blew out a breath. "Yeah. I think so."

"Max?"

"Max is dead."

"I hate it," he said groggily, "but there was no other choice." He winced when he tried to shrug. "How's Jason?"

"I have no idea. I checked on you first," I admitted and immediately regretted it.

"You like me, don't you?" Silas grinned, then chuckled when I rolled my eyes and pushed his head gently to the side.

I stood and made my way over to Jason. I made quick work of untying his hands and feet then rolled him onto his back as gently as I could. He stirred and then cupped a hand over his nose and mouth. "Son-of-a..."

"Yeah, I know it hurts, but you're alive, so suck it up." I smiled down at him.

Jason looked up at me and groaned. "As gentle as ever, Barb."

"We need to call the police." Silas sat up and leaned himself against the wall.

I nodded. "I'll do it."

I crawled over to Max and shoved my hand into his pocket. I found his and my cell phones. I powered mine on and pressed the speed-dial button to call Tyler.

The door to the bedroom burst open, and Tyler barged into the room like a madman, gun drawn and at the ready.

Silas, Jason, and I looked at each other, then at him with bored expressions.

"You're a little late, big guy." I pocketed my phone, stood, stepped over Jason, and made my way over to him.

"We got it covered." I patted his chest and smiled. I wasn't ready to admit to him, or even to myself for that matter, that we almost didn't have it covered and were well on our way to being dead with a capital D.

"What in the hell happened here?" Tyler looked around at the room. "Are you all right?" he lowered his gun and shoved it into the holster at his side under his arm.

"Well, Max there went insane." I pointed at Max's dead body on the floor. "He kidnapped us and then tried to kill us. As it turns out, he's your killer, not Jason." I motioned toward a very bloody Jason. He'd sat up and leaned his back against the dresser. "How'd you know where to find us?"

Tyler reached out and pulled me close to him, then started inspecting me as a mother would a child. It felt so weird and yet comforting. There might have been something more between Tyler and me than simple attraction after all.

Once he was satisfied that I wasn't seriously injured, he shoved his fingers through his hair and blew out a breath, then explained. "When I showed up at your place for our date the door was open. I knew something wasn't right. I went in and looked around and discovered that you were gone. There was a spot of blood on your bedroom floor, and your cat was freaking out."

"I'm fine." I assured him. "Max hit me in the head with his gun, and then he drugged me and brought me out here. Apparently he drugged all three of us." I motioned to Silas and Jason. "Is my cat okay?"

Tyler looked at me like I should be worried about something other than my cat, but he didn't know me well enough just yet to know that Mickey was family.

"He's fine. He's at Mandy's."

"How? And again, how'd you know to look for me here?"

"After I called the station to report your house being broken into and you missing, I called Kelly, and she called Mandy. That's how Mandy ended up with your cat. As for finding you, Mandy used the Find My Phone app installed on your phone, and it led here. I called for backup and paramedics as soon as we pinpointed your location. They'll be here any minute."

I could already hear the sirens.

"What exactly happened here, and who is Max?" Tyler pointed to Max.

"It's a long story." I sighed. "All you need to know at this moment is that he's Lydia's killer. Not Jason."

Tyler pressed a small black circle on his collar that I assumed was his com system, called an all clear to the other officers, and advised that paramedics were needed on the second floor.

He then reached out, pulled me into his arms, and held me. I melted against his chest. I didn't care that we were standing in the room with a dead body, a gigolo, and my lying, cheating ex-fiancé. In that moment I felt like I was right where I needed to be. In Tyler's protective embrace.

"Not your boyfriend, huh?" Silas chuckled from his spot against the wall.

I turned and gave him a *shut-it-or-I'll-shut-it-for-you* look, but in true Silas fashion, he just laughed.

"I understand your need to embrace that beautiful woman," Silas said. "But I could use some assistance over here." He hissed in a pained breath and motioned to his bloody arm.

"And my face is killing me, so could you wrap it up, Barb?" Jason mumbled a complaint from where he'd propped himself up against the dresser.

"Good grief. You two are such babies," I grumbled.

Two officers and a group of paramedics entered the room and descended on Silas and Jason. The two groaned and hissed as their wounds were examined.

I shook my head.

"What a bunch of whiners." I'd been in a car wreck, had my head bashed in, been drugged, kidnapped, and in a fight with a murderer all within the last twenty-four hours, and they didn't see my whining.

CHAPTER TWELVE

———

Two weeks had passed since I'd been kidnapped by Lydia's murderer.

In the meantime, the police dug deeper into Max's past and learned that over the years he'd had several restraining orders filed against him by a handful of different girlfriends when he lived in another state.

Turned out, he was deceptively charming and quite violent when the feeling suited him. Apparently Lydia wasn't the first to get under his skin, just the first he'd ever succeeded in murdering. I felt bad for him in a way that I couldn't really explain. Maybe he really did love Lydia, and maybe he was just insane. We'd never know.

Jason, Silas, and I were bandaged and cleared to leave by the hospital. Doctor Hope wasn't all that surprised to see me again, nor was he surprised to see Tyler hovering over me. At the station we gave our statements and answered the same questions what felt like a million times.

I was a bit worried that Silas would be in trouble for his gigolo business, but as it turned out, he wasn't promising sex to his clients. The only thing his company promised was an escort and a little fun, which could have meant anything, so he and his guys were in the clear.

The fact that he gave them wild monkey love anyway was apparently beside the point. I was glad that he wasn't in trouble. Silas and I had become good friends over the past couple of weeks, and I was thinking of using him on future cases as a decoy if the opportunity presented itself. With the number of cheating wives I dealt with, I was sure I'd be needing his assistance more often than not.

Tyler and I had seen each other as much as our jobs allowed since the night he found me standing over the dead body of a gigolo. We took it as a promising sign that we weren't sick of each other yet. I woke up every morning wanting to see him a little more than the day before.

He even sent me *Good morning, beautiful* texts every day.

"So, what does the handsome detective have planned for the two of you tonight?" Kelly waggled her eyebrows at me.

I applied a thin layer of mascara and placed the lid back on the container.

"Dinner and a movie at his place. He worked today, and you know me. I'd rather stay in than go out."

Kelly propped her feet up on the end of my bed and laced her fingers behind her head. Mickey took that as an invitation to join her and curled up against her side. She petted him idly. "You two were made for each other." She laughed.

"Why would you say that?" I asked as I slid my feet into a pair of pink sandals.

"You're both workaholics, hate going out somewhere crowded, and well, not to be mean, but you're a bit boring."

I laughed. "Boring? Tyler catches murderers for a living, and as of two weeks ago, so do I. Not to mention our new stud friend, Silas. After all of that, how can you say we're boring?" I grinned and propped my hands on my hips.

Kelly chuckled. "Believe me, you just are."

I shook my head and finished getting ready for my date. I supposed Tyler and I were boring to some people, but it didn't bother me one little bit.

"I still can't believe you freed yourself with a porn DVD." Kelly laughed and rubbed Mickey's belly. He looked up at her and purred.

"When all else fails..." I chuckled. "What other choice did I have at the time? Max was about to kill us."

"And that would've been a major shame." She shook her head. "I love you and all, but that Silas is one hot piece of—"

"I'm just going to stop you right there." I held up a hand. "If you like him that much, you could always pay the fee and have a go at that hot piece."

She rolled her eyes. "How does Tyler feel about you and Silas becoming such good friends?"

"He's okay with it." I shrugged my shoulders. "He wasn't at first, but it's all good now." And it really was. Tyler hadn't liked the idea of Silas and me getting close after what had just happened with Max and the kisses we'd shared, but with a little lip action and my promise that I was only interested in him, he gave me the benefit of the doubt and toned down the jealousy.

It still amazed me that someone as hot and amazing as Tyler could be interested in little plump me.

"I need to get going. Lock up when you let yourself out."

Kelly hopped up off the bed much to Mickey's displeasure and followed me into the living room. "I'm on my way out too. Mark is waiting for me at his place."

We stepped out onto the front porch, and I locked the door behind me.

"You two made up, I guess?"

Kelly and Mark were on-again, off-again more than a pair of panties in Silas's bedroom.

"Yeah. Everything is all right with us now. We just needed some time apart."

I'm not sure how that could be, as they were apart more than they were together, but it was none of my business. I was still getting the hang of this whole dating thing. Fortunately for me, Tyler was a very understanding man.

"Have fun. Try not to get too wild," Kelly called to me as she made her way to her car.

I sent her a one-fingered salute, and she laughed, got into her car, and drove away grinning.

I stepped down the stairs and couldn't help but smile at the car sitting in my driveway. As of this morning, my days of driving the pea-soup wagon were officially over. Thanks to the insurance company and the increase in income from Jason's case, as well as some others I'd signed, I was now the proud owner of the black Cadillac CTS that I'd wanted. Since wrapping up Lydia's case, clients were flooding the office, and I didn't have to worry about paying the light bill anymore.

I slipped into my new car, sighed with pleasure at the new-car smell, and pulled out of the driveway.

I had a hunky detective waiting for me.

* * *

I pulled into Tyler's driveway and was a bit surprised to see the house was mostly dark.

I got out of the car and bumped the door shut with my hip, then shoved my keys into my bag.

I was beginning to wonder if he'd cancelled our date, and I'd missed the message, but when I reached the steps leading up to his front door, I froze in my tracks.

A trail of coffee-flavored hard candy and my favorite watermelon bubblegum led to the partially open door.

What was going on? Did Tyler have some kind of big plan that I wasn't aware of or ready for? I had the odd urge to turn around and run back to my car, but at the same time, I needed to find out what was going on.

I pushed the door open and saw that the trail continued into the living area. I followed the trail of goodies a few more feet then stopped.

I laughed.

"This is awesome."

The candy trail ended in the living room. Right in front of the television was a picnic-style dinner of pizza, beer, and even an after-dinner iced caramel macchiato with my name written on the cup...literally.

Tyler looked up from where he was already seated on the red-and-black plaid blanket and grinned.

He had the most devastating grin. I think my heart skipped a beat.

"So you approve?"

"More than approve," I said, then set my purse on the couch and knelt down beside him.

He leaned over and ran his thumb down my cheek, then tipped my head up, and kissed my lips. Just the simplest touch from Tyler could make my toes curl.

"Kelly informed me that we're boring," he said. "And since neither one of us cares for fancy restaurants or nightclubs, I thought I'd do something that we'd both enjoy. So"—he spread his arms out—"picnic dinner, dessert, and cheesy movies."

"She told me the same thing earlier." I laughed. "You have no idea how perfect this is," I assured him.

He dropped his arms and brushed my hair behind my ear. "Honestly, we've both been working such long hours, I just wanted to get you all to myself for as long as possible."

My chest ached from his sweetness.

In all of my thirty years, I'd never been with a man who made me feel the way Tyler did. He was strong, confident, gentle, caring, loyal, and even though he could go overboard with it at times, protective. Tyler was everything I'd ever wanted in a man, and it was still hard for me to believe that he wanted me. That he liked me just the way I was.

I looked around at the simple, yet incredibly thoughtful, setting and then at his beautiful, hopeful face and smiled.

In that moment, I knew that I was right where I belonged.

I leaned over and gave Tyler a soft kiss on his firm, plump lips, then leaned back and met his heated gaze.

"You can have me for as long as you want me, Detective. There's nowhere else I'd rather be."

ABOUT THE AUTHOR

Not only is Anna Snow a wife, mom, and lipstick junkie, but she's also a multi-published bestselling author of several romance, mystery, erotica, fan-fiction, paranormal, chick-lit, and thriller works.

Anna began writing as soon as she could hold a pen and hasn't stopped since. She loves life and can think of nothing she enjoys more than spending time with her family and friends. She loves reading, kitties, spending time outdoors, and did I mention kitties? *Big grin* Anna also loves to hear from her fans and answers all correspondence she receives.

To learn more about Anna, visit her online at
www.annasnow.info

Enjoyed this book? Check out these other fun reads available in print now from Gemma Halliday Publishing:

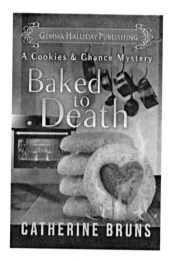

CPSIA information can be obtained
at www.ICGtesting.com
Printed in the USA
LVOW12s1711060716

495333LV00001B/117/P

9 781523 652723

OKANAGAN REGIONAL LIBRARY

3 3132 03894 7182